# Connected by the Sea

Copyright © 2013 by E. L. Todd

All Rights Reserved

ISBN-13: 978-1494480585

ISBN-10: 1494480581

# Connected by the Sea

Book One of the Hawaiian Crush Series

E. L. Todd

As soon as the other employees left Hawaiian Sea Life, clocking out from their evening shifts at the aquarium, Sydney shut down all the lights before she walked down the hall. A large tank was on her left side. Tropical fish and a few small sharks comprised the sealed underwater terrain. An eel was in the crevasse of a rock, its head poking out. His eyes were watching the fish swim by, interested in their presence. The ecology of that tank was more breathtaking than watching people walk through Union Square in San Francisco, a place she used to visit often when she lived in California. Sydney had always been fascinated by the life below the surface of the ocean. If she had to choose between discovering the secrets of the ocean, or the unknown of space, the sea would win every time.

Bubbles floated to the surface from the soil below, and the seaweed swayed in the fake tide. When she reached the end of the hallway, she slid her card through the scanner then walked inside. Her friends were already waiting.

"Take a seat," Henry said as he handed her a beer.

She sat down in the lawn chair next to him. It was old and rusty with a major hole in the seat of it. All the tools on the deck area were ancient and worn out. "Thanks, my friend."

He held up his beer and smiled. "You're most welcome."

Nancy was leaning back in her chair. "I thought that day would never end."

Sydney sighed. "Who knew fish could be so dirty? I didn't know they pooped so much."

"Those penguins must have eaten some bad fish because they had loads of diarrhea," Henry said with a disgusted face.

Sydney had her beer pressed to her lips but she decided to put it down. Just imagining the smell curbed her thirst. "At least it's over." She looked across the dolphin pool and out to the ocean. The aquarium sat on a cliff face that overlooked the coast. The colors purple and orange mixed together to form a breathtaking sky. The humid wind brushed through her hair and made her relax. She loved living in Hawaii. She was never going to leave.

Henry looked at her, leaning his head back. "Ready for the exam?"

She shrugged. "I guess."

He rolled his eyes. "You'll probably get the highest score, like usual."

She narrowed her eyes at him. "I told you to stop looking at my scores."

"I can't help it. I sit right next to you."

"Well, don't sit next to me anymore."

"Then how am I supposed to copy you?" he asked with a smile.

"If you copy me and still fail, there must be some serious issues going on in your brain."

"I won't argue with that."

Nancy yawned. "I want to change my major."

"To what?" Sydney asked.

"Zoology. Molecular biology totally sucks." She drank from her beer.

"What were you expecting?" Henry asked.

Nancy shook her head. "I studied so hard for that class and still got a B. It's not my thing."

"I think it was the instructor," Henry said. "It seemed like she used random slides from other places, like the textbook or some education site and didn't understand what she was reading." He drank from his beer then put it down. "That tuition money was well spent."

Sydney laughed. "Most definitely."

The three of them fell silent as they listened to the crashing waves. The fin of a dolphin could be seen on the surface of the water every few minutes.

"Did you feed them?" Sydney asked.

Henry nodded. "Of course. They were practically screaming at me when I opened the door."

"They are so smart."

Nancy leaned forward and looked into the water. "And really cute."

Henry rolled his eyes. "They look just like fish."

"I think they are cute too," Sydney said as she stared at the water.

Henry was quiet for a moment. "Yeah. They are."

Sydney finished her can then dropped it into her lap. "I guess we should clock out now."

"We're such good workers," Henry said.

"Well, being a janitor sucks," Nancy said. "We deserve some lounging time."

"I hope I get promoted soon," Sydney said. "I've been doing this for two years now."

Henry placed his hand on her shoulder then gripped it. "You'll get there."

She sighed. "Yeah."

They grabbed the lawn chairs then stacked them in the corner. They put their beers cans in Nancy's purse so they wouldn't be found by the wrong people.

Sydney kneeled down at the pool's edge and looked into the water. A dolphin broke the surface and screeched at her.

"Hello, Rose," Sydney said as she rubbed the slippery flesh of the dolphin's forehead. "How are you?"

Rose kicked her tail and continued to screech.

"That's good to hear."

3

Henry approached her and kneeled next to her. He said nothing while he watched her pet the dolphin. He noticed the look of love in Sydney's eyes. He reached out and placed his hand on the cold flesh and stroked the dolphin gently.

Sydney paid no attention to him. Her eyes were on her companion. "I wish I could swim with you today."

The dolphin moved out of the water a little more, sticking her nose toward Sydney's face. Sydney reached down and kissed the dolphin between the eyes. "Goodnight."

The dolphin pulled away and disappeared under the water.

Henry stared at her, watching her eyes reflect the light of the heavens. "It's like she understands you."

"She does understand me."

"If you say so," he said with a laugh." He stood up then grabbed her hand, helping her to her feet. "Let's go."

Sydney waved at the pool before they left the outside alcove and entered the main building. They walked to the locker room and changed before they clocked out for the day. Sydney was relieved to don her shorts and thin shirt. She hated wearing the bulky, heavy clothes required for work.

After setting the building alarm, they walked outside to the parking lot.

Nancy nudged Sydney in the ribs. "Bonfire this weekend?"

"Yeah. Sounds like fun."

"I'm surprised you can squeeze it in. It seems like you're always so busy."

She shrugged. "I'll sleep when I'm dead."

Nancy stopped when she reached her old Camaro. "I'll see you tomorrow."

"Night," Sydney said with a wave.

Henry nodded to her.

Sydney approached her Jeep Wrangler, which had no doors, and threw her bag in the passenger seat. The wind picked up and blew the strands of her brown hair from her neck. She could smell the flowers and leaves in the air, mixed with the salt spray of the sea. She loved living in paradise. She felt safe on the island, hidden from the rest of the world.

"Can I come over?" Henry asked.

"Sure," Sydney said with a shrug. "But I'm tired. I don't feel like doing anything."

"Not even studying?" he teased.

"I can't study anymore," she said with a heavy breath.

"That's fine. I wouldn't mind watching a movie."

"You really hate your roommates, huh?"

"They are just loud and messy. I like sex as much as the next guy, but I get tired of hearing the headboard slam against my wall in the middle of the night."

"I love living alone."

"I'm jealous. Let me know if you ever want a roommate."

"A male roommate?" she asked with a raised eyebrow.

"I'm there all the time anyway."

"I guess."

"So it's cool?"

"Yeah. I'll see you there."

Henry smiled. "I'll see you soon, Syd."

She climbed into her Jeep then started the engine. A few of her friends, particularly Henry, warned her about not having any doors, but she wasn't worried about it. She was an excellent driver and always paid attention to the road. Plus, she loved having a vehicle that was so open to the elements. The wind would brush through her hair and the sun would beat on her skin. She couldn't imagine driving anything else.

She left the aquarium and drove through the suburbs until she reached the tiny house she owned on a small plot of land. It was walking distance from the beach, and she could hear the ocean waves through her window. It wasn't a nice place, pretty run down, but it was the closest thing she would ever come find near the beach. She couldn't have asked for a better inheritance.

After she parked her Jeep, Henry pulled up in his Mazda a moment later.

"So what should we watch?" he asked as he walked with her to the front door.

She shrugged. "It doesn't matter. We probably won't watch it anyway."

Henry was quiet for a moment. He looked at her, hope on his face. "We won't?"

"I'll probably fall asleep."

"Oh."

She unlocked the door and they walked inside. Sydney tossed her backpack by the front door then entered the living room. Henry sat down on the couch and turned on the television.

Sydney grabbed a glass of water then lay on the opposite couch. She pulled a blanket over herself then sighed.

Henry stared at her, watching her brown hair lay across the pillow. After a moment, he returned his gaze to the screen. "Can I sleep here tonight?"

"You're always welcome here, Henry."

"Thanks."

"Is it Mitch?"

He nodded. "He's an ass."

"You want me to talk to him?"

Henry shook his head. "Don't worry about it, Syd. I can take care of it."

"If you're over here all the time, you obviously can't."

"Maybe I just like being over here."

She laughed. "Yeah, okay."

"What? I like being with you."

"Well, I'm the lesser of two evils."

"Or you're just the coolest person I know."

She tightened the blanket around her shoulder. "Can you set the alarm? I'm about to fall asleep."

"Sure." He pulled out his phone and set the clock. After a few minutes, he rose from the couch then kneeled before her. He pressed his lips against her brow and ran his fingers through her hair, enjoying the silky feel. He stared at her for a long time before he closed his eyes, saddened that she didn't even notice him. She would never notice him.

## 2

When the alarm went off, Sydney rolled on her side and moaned.

Henry shook her leg. "Come on. We have an exam today."

"Don't remind me."

He rolled his eyes. "You ace every exam. You don't have to worry about anything."

"I would still rather sleep than take a test."

He laughed. "Come on, Syd."

She sighed then sat up. Her hair was a tangled mess as she ran her fingers through the heap on top of her head. "I need two minutes." She walked in the bathroom and fixed her hair before she changed into denim shorts and a halter top. She loved living on Oahu because she was never cold. It was shorts, flip-flops, and t-shirts all year. She never wore any makeup so she walked out the door with Henry. He usually brought a change of clothes when he stayed at Sydney's place. He was there so often that she considered asking him to move in with her. Henry disliked having roommates because of all the bullshit that went along with it, but she wasn't sure how she felt about living with a guy, even if he was a good friend.

"Don't skip breakfast," Henry said as he tossed her a banana.

She caught it. "Thanks, Mommy."

He smiled. "You're welcome, princess." He got into his car then shut the door.

Sydney threw her backpack in the seat before she climbed inside. When she pulled out of the dirt driveway, she headed to the main road and drove to the campus of University of Hawaii. She found a parking spot and Henry parked right next to her.

"Why don't we just carpool?" he asked.

She climbed out of the Jeep then walked across the grass with him. "Because we have other things to do."

"We could drop each other off."

"Nah." Sydney liked being around Henry, but she felt like he wanted to spend even more time together than they already did. It surprised her. She didn't think she was that interesting. Henry was much taller than her at six feet. His brown hair was dark like hers, and he had a slight tan from the shining sun. He was thin and toned with a perfectly straight smile and pearly white teeth. She loved seeing him smile when she made him laugh. That grin was definitely his best feature.

When they walked into the building, students were still studying their notes as they stood outside, cramming at the last minute.

Henry shrugged. "What's the point? I'm going to fail anyway."

"Then why did you pick this major?"

He stared at the students who were scanning their textbooks and outlines, saying nothing for a long time. "I enjoy it."

They walked inside and took their seats in the third row like they did every day. Sydney looked over and spotted Coen sitting alone. He was leaning back in his chair, staring straight ahead. Even though he wasn't behaving differently, she knew there was something bothering him. His arms were crossed over his chest and his muscles were tighter than usual. His short brown hair was curly at the ends, flipping up slightly. His blue eyes reminded her of the ocean, deep and mysterious. She always thought his body was fascinating. His arms were large but not too big, and his torso was flat with defined muscles. Whenever he moved his arms, she could see the muscles of his back stretch and recoil, showing all the lines and definitions even through his shirt. A tattoo marked his forearm. It looked like a tribal dog. He was definitely the type of guy she shouldn't be attracted to, but she knew she was. Her lips always opened when she looked at him, wondering what it would be like to taste his lips with her tongue. But there was no possibility of anything happening between them. He had a girlfriend, and even if he didn't, he wasn't the right guy for her. He was a player. Still, it didn't hurt just to look.

"Syd?"

"Huh?"

"Do you have an extra pencil I can use?"

"Oh...yeah...sure." She dug in her backpack while Henry stared at the object of her desire. He hated Coen. He never spoke to the guy in his life, but he still hated him. Why couldn't Sydney look at him in the same way? With lust? Why didn't she notice him? As much as he hated to admit it, he was jealous. She came back up and handed the pencil to Henry. "Here."

"Thanks," he said quietly.

Nancy came into the room and sat beside Sydney. "Are you ready for this?"

Sydney shrugged. "It's just a test. The more you stress about it, the worse you're going to do."

Nancy rolled her eyes then looked at Henry. "I can't even talk to her sometimes."

"Yeah," he said with a laugh.

Sydney crossed her arms over her chest and faced forward. The rest of the students filed into their seats right when the teacher walked inside.

"You guys ready?" Professor Jones asked.

There was absolute silence.

"I'll take that as a yes," he said as he pulled the exams from his bag. "I like the enthusiasm."

Sydney chuckled to herself. She always understood his humor.

He licked his fingertips then started passing the sheets down each row. "Please don't start until everyone has a copy." Sydney snuck one more glance at Coen. He rubbed his eyes with his fingers before Professor Jones told them to begin.

Sydney went through the multiple choice questions with ease and found her answers quickly. She finished the essay portion then began her practical exam, which took place in the back of the room. She identified the different parts of the specimens while Professor Jones nodded to her in approval, knowing she was proficient in her abilities. When she was done, she was the first to submit her exam before turning to leave. When she looked at Coen, his face was buried in his hands. His test was completely blank. Without another look, she walked out.

She advanced down the hall until she reached the sitting area, a place sectioned off for students to study in the science building. Sydney pulled out the banana Henry gave her and ate it while waiting for her friends to finish their test.

Coen walked out a moment later. His back was straight and his shoulders square. He looked how he always looked, confident and stern, but his eyes were empty. He stared at her for a moment before he walked away. Sydney knew he failed the exam. There was no way he finished that quickly, and if he did, he must have guessed the entire time. Pity rose in her heart. She knew he wasn't stupid, so she didn't understand why he was struggling.

Henry and Nancy appeared a few minutes later.

"How'd it go?" she asked.

Henry took the banana from her hand, took a bite, then returned it to her. "I think I passed," he said after he swallowed.

Nancy crossed her arms over her chest. "And I hope I passed."

"Why don't you study with me during open lab? I can help both of you," Sydney offered.

Henry shook his head. "We aren't on the same—level. When you explain things to me I'm just confused the whole time."

Sydney narrowed her eyes. "I'm speaking English."

"But I still don't get it."

"It's pure memorization," she snapped back. "You just have to do the work. You aren't putting in the effort."

Nancy shook her head. "We aren't as intelligent as you are."

"I hate it when people say that. People are intelligent in different ways. I have a more mathematical and logical mind. Henry is more of a language person. He can always speak elegantly and form ideas without any issues. He can read Shakespeare and understand it perfectly. Nancy, you see things in art that I never see."

Henry raised an eyebrow. "So you're saying that I should be an English major and Nancy should change her major to art?"

"No," she said in frustration. "You just learn differently than I do. I see something and I just get it. Henry, you need to read and talk to yourself out loud. Nancy, you should draw pictures of what you see."

Nancy was quiet for a moment. "I guess I could try that."

Henry nodded. "And I can just read the textbook."

"Or you can change your major to English," she teased.

"Maybe I should," he said.

"I'll support whatever you want to do. Don't study zoology if you don't like it."

Henry looked at her but said nothing.

Nancy sat down at the table. "What do you guys want to do now?"

I shrugged. "Take a nap."

"That doesn't sound bad," Henry said.

"We do have the bonfire tonight," Nancy said. "We need to be rested for that."

"Let's finish our classes then head back to my place," Sydney offered.

"I wonder when Jones will have the exams back," Henry said.

Sydney tossed the banana peel in the trash. "Monday."

Henry shook his head. "I hope not."

"Did you see Coen?" Nancy asked. "His entire exam was blank."

Sydney looked up. "It was? The whole thing?" She had hoped that he at least tried to guess. It was a twenty-five percent chance he got his answers right. It was better than nothing.

Henry noticed the concern in her eyes. "He obviously doesn't care so why should we?"

Nancy shrugged. "Maybe something happened to him."

"He could've just told Jones and rescheduled the exam if that were the case," Henry said. He looked at Sydney. "He's a loser."

Sydney met his gaze but said nothing.

"Well, I have English," Nancy said as she walked away. "I'll see you later."

"I wish I had English," Henry said with a grin. "Bye."

Nancy waved. "Bye."

Henry looked at Sydney. "Are you ready for physio?"

"Yeah," she said with a sigh. "I can't believe we have all the same classes this semester again."

He shrugged. "What a coincidence."

They walked into their physio class and took a seat in the back. Sydney was tired from the exam she just took so she wasn't taking as many notes as usual. Henry wasn't taking any at all. He normally typed away on his laptop but that wasn't the case today. After the class was done, they walked back to the parking lot.

"Your place?" Henry asked with a smile.

"Why don't we ever go to yours?"

"You remember all the stories, right? That place is practically a brothel."

"Maybe they would behave differently if a friendly girl was there."

He shook his head rapidly. "They would gang up on you like a pack of wolves."

"Talk about raging hormones."

"Yeah."

"Why don't you have girls over all the time?"

He ran his fingers through his hair. "I just haven't found anyone I like."

"Is that why they're mean to you?"

He sighed. "They keep saying I'm gay."

"Are you?"

He looked hurt. The light disappeared from his eyes. "I'm definitely not gay."

Sydney stared at his chest. He was wide and strong, and his flat stomach was noticeable through his shirt. He had long legs and muscled thighs. Henry was a hot guy, someone that most girls were attracted to. Sydney was surprised that he didn't sleep around with all the women he could get. "I just never hear you talk about girls you think are hot."

"Well, that's disrespectful."

"How?"

"It's disrespectful to you."

"I'm not following."

"You're a girl. You really want to hear me say which girls I'd like to fuck?"

"It wouldn't bother me."

His eyes lost even more light. He opened his car door and averted his gaze. "I'm not feeling well. I'll see you at the bonfire later." He shut the door, started the engine, then took off. Sydney stayed by her Jeep, lost in thought. She didn't know what she said to offend him, but she obviously said something. Since they spent so much time together, she wondered why they didn't talk about sex or potential partners. It was something they never discussed. She thought it was weird.

She climbed into her Jeep then left the parking lot. After she drove through the suburbs, she parked in her driveway under the trees and saw that Nancy had already arrived. Her class must have gotten out early.

"Hey. What took so long?"

"Henry and I were talking."

"Where is he?" Nancy asked.

"He decided to go home."

"Is everything okay?"

"I don't know," Sydney said as she walked to the front door and unlocked it. "I asked him about girls and he got all weird. Sometimes I wonder if he's gay but he's too afraid to admit it, like I'll judge him or something."

Nancy smiled. "Henry is definitely straight."

"Then why did he act like that?" She placed her backpack on the floor then walked into the living room with her friend trailing behind her.

"What did you say exactly?"

"I said I didn't care if he checked out girls and talked about fucking them—something like that. Then he just took off."

Nancy nodded but said nothing.

"Weird, right?"

"Uh—yeah." She had a different expression on her face, like she was trying not to fart.

"Are you not telling me something?"

She turned away. "No."

"Nancy?"

"I don't know why he acted that way," she said quickly. "I'm not as close to Henry as you are. Maybe you should just ask him next time you see him."

"Maybe I will," she said.

"Okay." She walked into the kitchen and started making a margarita. "You want one, right?"

"So we are going to get drunk before the bonfire?"

"Well, I am."

"I guess I'll be the designated driver tonight."

"Duh." She added the ingredients and turned on the blender.

Sydney went into her room and changed into yellow shorts with a white tube top. She wore a dangling golden necklace the held a pendent of a dolphin. Then, she curled her hair and teased it, making it big and wavy. When she walked out to the back porch to join Nancy, her friend eyed her in approval.

"You look hot," she said.

Sydney laughed. "I just did my hair."

"You should do it like that every day."

"No. Too much work." Sydney grabbed the drink from the table and started to sip it. There wasn't much wind and the waves were docile. The moon was nowhere in sight as the sun went down.

"We should leave soon," Nancy said.

"Yeah."

"So, speaking of dating people."

"When were we talking about dating people?"

"When we were talking about Henry."

"Oh. Are you seeing anyone?"

"No. Is there anyone you like?"

She was quiet for a moment. Coen popped into her mind. "No. Not really."

"Not really?"

"There's no one I have any real interest in. I think a few guys are cute but that's it."

"So you aren't over Aaron?"

Sydney drank half the glass then put it down. "I'm definitely over him."

"I would hope so. It's been six months."

"Yeah."

"So why haven't you moved on?"

"I have moved on."

She rolled her eyes. "Why haven't you started dating?"

"I would if I saw someone I liked."

"How will you know unless you start going out?"

"Well, going on random dates doesn't sound productive either."

"Don't you need to get laid?"

Sydney glared at her. "Are we really going to do this?"

"I'm just trying to help you get back on the horse."

"When I see someone I like, I'll ride him, okay?"

She laughed. "Okay." She spun her straw around her glass and avoided Sydney's look. "How about Henry? He's cute."

"He's my friend."

"So?"

"I don't see him like that."

"Well, I think he's hot."

"Then why don't you date him?"

She glared at me. "I know how to get back on the horse. We are trying to help *you* here."

"By ruining my friendship with him?"

"Why would it be ruined?"

"Because when friends date and break up, they're never friends again. It would just be awkward."

"Is that the only reason you won't date him?"

"No. I don't see him like that."

She drank from her straw. "Oh."

"And Henry doesn't see me like that either."

Nancy laughed into her straw and the margarita came out her nose.

Sydney looked at her. "What's so funny?"

She wiped her face with her napkin. "Nothing."

"Nancy?"

"I was just thinking about something that happened earlier today."

She narrowed her eyes in suspicion but didn't comment.

"Do you think Coen is cute?"

Sydney smiled. "He's a good-looking guy."

"Doesn't he have a girlfriend?"

Her smile dropped. "Yes."

"So, he's out."

"I wouldn't date him anyway."

"Why?"

"I can tell what kind of guy he is. He's a heartbreaker and a player. Definitely not trustworthy."

"So the only guy you're interested in is a total ass?"

She sighed. "What's wrong with me?"

"First Aaron and now this guy. You sure know how to pick em."

"I know, right?"

Nancy looked at her watch. "Let's go."

Sydney finished the rest of her glass then followed behind her.

# 3

There were five controlled fires scattered along the beach. The small parking lot was already crammed with cars, so they parked along the sand like everyone else. It was dark outside but the bonfires acted as a bright beacon, more powerful than the lighthouses that called lost ships to shore. The other students were frolicking along the sand, throwing footballs to one another, drinking beer from the ice chest, or making out in the sand. Sydney spotted one couple lying under a blanket on the sand. It was obvious they were having sex by the way they were moving. She missed having sex on a regular basis. It was odd when something you had every day just stopped.

They climbed from the Jeep then walked down the sand. When they passed different groups near the fire, the men stared at Sydney and Nancy, pleased by what they saw.

"They must like your hair too," Nancy said.

Sydney ignored her comment. She knew she wasn't ugly but she didn't think she was pretty either. Her legs were a little larger than the usual skinny girl. She had muscles from her training and her swimming exercises. She was thicker than most girls her size. She had a petite frame and a tiny body, but had more muscle tone than normal. Her stomach was flat and defined. Sometimes Sydney wondered if she looked a little too muscular, but she didn't care what people thought. She would rather be slightly bulky than thin and frail. When she and Aaron made love, he always said he loved her body. But then again, perhaps he was just lying. She couldn't trust anything he said.

"There's Henry," Nancy said happily.

"I hope he isn't still acting weird."

"He probably wouldn't have come if he was."

They approached Henry and everyone else.

"I like the hair," Derek said, cocking his head to the side.

"Thanks," Sydney said. "It took me a long time. I'm glad someone noticed."

"It looks amazing," Henry blurted.

Sydney looked at him and smiled. "Thanks."

He smiled back. It seemed like they were back to normal.

Derek was the same height as Henry. He had blond hair and blue eyes, typical surfer. "I heard your zoology exam was brutal."

She shrugged. "It was okay."

"For you," Henry added.

"How are your classes going?" she asked Derek.

"They're going. I want to stay in school as long as possible. I never want to leave this place."

"Get your PhD in surfing," she said.

He laughed. "If only I could."

Laura walked over with two beers in her hand. "Here you are, honey," she said as she handed one to Sydney.

"Thanks," she said as she took it.

Henry grabbed the top and twisted the cap off.

"I can do it," she said.

"I wanted to save you the trouble," he said.

She turned back to Laura and hugged her. "How are you?"

"Good. I'm just glad it's Friday. I'm always happy on Friday." Laura was tall and thin with blonde hair that reached her breasts. She was very beautiful but couldn't stay in the sun for long without getting burned. She was one of the few people I knew who didn't like living on the island.

"Me too."

Derek laughed. "This is my Sunday night." He covered his face with his hands and looked like someone had just died. "Then this is me on Friday." He smiled wide and clicked his heels.

"Sundays are the worst," Henry said as he drank from his beer. He returned his gaze to Sydney and stared at her for a long time. When she looked back, she wondered how many beers he'd had. She could tell he was already buzzed.

"Sydney?"

She turned around, facing the ocean. "Aaron?"

"Hey," he said with his hands in his pockets. "I thought that was you."

She nodded. "How are you?"

He glanced down to the sand then returned his eyes to her face, looking crestfallen. He took a deep breath. "Good. I heard you had an exam today. I'm sure you aced it—like usual."

"Yeah. I'm glad it's over."

He stared at her for a long time. His brown hair was ruffled from the wind but it still looked nice. His wide shoulders always reminded her of their midnight fuckings. She loved his body. When she pictured him naked, she forced the thought from her mind. She was just lonely. The thoughts meant nothing.

"Can I talk to you for a second?" he asked.

"Uh—"

"Is he bothering you?" Henry asked as he wrapped his arm around her waist. He glared at Aaron. "Fuck off, you piece of shit." Everyone was looking at them now.

Sydney looked at Henry in shock. He really did have too much to drink. "It's okay, Henry."

"No, it's not. He keeps bothering you and I'm tired of it."

She pulled his hand from her waist then patted his shoulder. "I appreciate you looking out for me but I can take care of myself, okay?"

His eyes still held the rage, but he didn't say anything more.

Sydney left his side and joined Aaron. After they walked to the water and got their feet wet, he looked at her.

"He's had too much to drink, huh?"

"I'm sorry. I think he's drunk."

"I've never seen him act like that."

"He's been weird all day. Something is bothering him."

"I have a feeling it isn't just me." He let the waves wash over his feet.

The water felt warm even at that hour. This was the hottest ocean that Sydney had ever experienced. In California, the water was so cold she almost got hypothermia a few times. They told her to stay out of the water but she never listened. That was like asking a child not to stick his hand in the cookie jar. It couldn't be done. "So, what's up?"

He walked farther along the beach with his hands in his pockets, Sydney walking right beside him. "It's been six months, Syd."

"I know."

"I haven't been with anyone else, talked to anyone else, slept with anyone. I don't want anyone but you. I'm sorry about my stupid mistake. I would take it back if I could but I can't. Please give me another chance."

She continued to walk but said nothing. The light from the campfires was disappearing, leaving them in darkness. "We're over, Aaron. I'm sorry."

He closed his eyes and said nothing for a long time. "I've proven that you can trust me. Let me show you how much I've changed."

"You can't undo what you did."

He ran his fingers through his hair. "You never would have found out unless I told you the truth. I could have kept it from you and we would still be together right now, but I respected you too much to lie to you. Doesn't that mean something to you?" He stopped walking and grabbed her, holding her to his chest. "Doesn't it?"

She looked into his eyes then averted her gaze. "Yes, it does. But you still cheated on me. I can't stop picturing you with someone else. I can't be with someone that hurt me so much."

He grabbed her chin and directed her look on him. "I love you, baby. I'm sorry about what I did, but I was drunk and can't remember anything that happened. I just know that I fucked her. It meant absolutely nothing to me."

"Then why did you throw us away for it?"

He sighed. "I was drunk. It was a stupid mistake and I'll regret it for the rest of my life."

"I can't just let it go and pretend it didn't happen."

"I'm not asking you to. Just try again with me. Just try."

She was quiet for a long moment. "No."

"Don't you miss me? I miss you every day."

"I used to miss you. But now I miss the time we had together, not you as a person."

He cupped her face and held her forehead to his. "I can make you miss me. I can be everything you want me to be. All you have to do is let me try."

She wrapped her arms around his neck and closed her eyes. "You can keep asking me over and over but it will change nothing. I suggest you move on and find someone else. I'm not coming back. You already lost me. All you're doing is causing yourself more pain. I don't want you to be in pain."

He closed his eyes and held her close. A tear dripped from his eye but he wiped it away. Sydney closed her eyes, unable to watch any longer.

"Stop making me hurt you," she whispered.

He sniffed then kissed her on the forehead. "I know I don't deserve you but I want to deserve you."

"I'll always love you, Aaron."

"I love you, Sydney."

"Please stop chasing me."

He sighed. "There's nothing I can do?"

She shook her head. "I'm sorry."

He swallowed the lump in his throat. "Okay."

She looked at his lips and he looked at hers. The waves crashed over their feet and the wind rustled their hair. Sydney placed her hand on his chest and felt his heartbeat under her palm. It was as powerful as the tide. He placed his hand on her cheek then his thumb on her bottom lip. His blue eyes shined bright from the distant bonfires.

"I want to kiss you one last time."

She said nothing, wanting him to.

He rubbed his nose against hers then pressed his lips to her mouth. The heat of his skin made her shake. He slipped his tongue inside of her and she moaned at the feel of him. She had been celibate for six months and missed being touched like this. When she realized what she was doing and where it would lead, she pulled away.

His lips were still open, missing her. "Have you been with anyone since we broke up?"

"No."

"Do you miss it?"

She crossed her arms over chest, knowing exactly what he was asking. "Yes."

"I do too." He stared into her eyes, placing his hands in his pockets. "I would like to do that once more too."

She looked away. "That can't happen."

"Why? Just one more time. I'm tired of jerking off when I think about you."

His words made her skin tingle. "No. You know what will happen."

"What?"

"We'll get back together."

"And what's bad about that?"

"I don't want that."

"But you still love me."

"I'll always love you, Aaron. But it wouldn't mean anything."

"I'm okay with that."

"I'm not."

"Aren't you frustrated as hell?" he asked with a laugh. "I feel like I'm going crazy."

"I'm frustrated that you ruined something so beautiful to fuck some girl."

He sighed. "I wasn't in my right state of mind. I don't even remember it."

"That just makes it even better," she said sarcastically.

"I will do anything to win you back. Anything."

"Just leave me alone, Aaron."

"Let me make love to you. I'll prove how much I love you."

"No."

"Baby, please."

"I said no. I deserve someone better than you. You will never understand how much you hurt me." Tears sprang from her eyes. She wiped them away and hid them from his view. "I won't do it again. I can't. I loved you so much and you totally broke my heart. I want to be with someone that I know will never do that to me. That someone isn't you, Aaron."

"I wish it was."

"But it's not. And you should be with someone that you love so much you would never cheat on them."

"I wouldn't cheat on you."

"Well, I was the lesson that you learned. Now learn from your mistake and make someone else happy. That person isn't me."

"Is this really it?"

25

"It's been it, Aaron. We're done—over."

"I hate this."

"I do too."

"But you still love me."

"Not like I used to."

"Then why haven't you been with someone else? Or are you with Henry?"

"I'm not with Henry."

"Then you must still want me."

"No. I just can't sleep with someone else so quickly."

He closed his eyes, feeling the sting. "I deserved that."

She turned away from him then walked up the beach. "Please leave me alone. I can't move on if you still pull me back. If you love me, you'll let me go."

He joined her on the beach then walked alongside her. "That's so hard."

"You have to."

He was quiet for a moment. "Okay." He grabbed her hand and held it in his own. "But you're still mine for the next minute."

She squeezed his hand but said nothing. When they got back to the bonfires, he turned to her and hugged her tightly. She didn't release him and he didn't let her go for a long time. Henry stood by and watched them.

When they pulled away, Aaron kissed her on the forehead. "Whoever gets to keep you is the luckiest man in the world." He turned away and walked past the fires until he reached the parking lot. Sydney said nothing for a very long time. Henry wrapped his arm around her shoulder and held her close.

"Are you okay?" he whispered, alcohol heavy on his breath.

"Yes. He's finally letting me go."

"We'll see."

She said nothing.

Henry gripped her waist and pulled her into his chest, holding her tightly. She placed her head on his shoulder and wrapped her arms around his neck, relaxing in his embrace. Nancy and the others huddled close to them but said nothing. They were all there when the breakup happened and knew how much it hurt Sydney. Henry knew it best of all.

"I got you," he whispered.

"I know," she said. "Thank you for being my friend."

He stiffened at her words. "Yeah."

She pulled away. "I'm okay. I'm just going to get a drink."

"I can get it," he said quickly.

She smiled. "Please. Allow me."

He stepped back and let her go.

She walked past the fires until she came to an ice chest. It was totally empty. She moved to the next one and dug through the frozen ice until she found a bottle of beer at the bottom. When she heard yelling, she looked up.

Coen was gripping his hair while he spoke to his girlfriend. His tattoo flashed in the light of the flames. She kept wrapping her arms around him, trying to kiss him, but he kept dodging her affections. When he tried to walk away, she held him still. When he tried to move again, she slapped him across the face. Coen stilled for a moment, anger spewing from his eyes but he didn't retaliate. He turned away again.

"Coen!"

"Let me go," he snapped. He marched from the beach then headed toward the parking lot. She kept following him, crying the entire way.

Sydney felt sorry for the girl. She probably caught him cheating, and now he just wanted to get away from her. Or he just dumped her after he told her he loved her just so he could sleep with her. She was hurt by Aaron, but at least she didn't have to suffer through that. A part of her believed that Aaron really did love her, but it wasn't enough for her. She needed something more.

# 4

Sydney went home and Henry followed right behind her. She told him to leave, that she would be fine alone, but he insisted. When they walked inside, Sydney washed her face and put on her pajamas before she walked into the living room. Henry was already lying on the couch with the blanket over him.

"Good night," she said as she turned off all the lights.

"Sydney?"

"Hmm?"

"You okay?"

"I'm fine, Henry."

"You guys talked for a long time."

"We repeated everything that was already said."

"You're never getting back together?"

She ran her fingers through her hair then sighed. "No."

He nodded. "I'm glad. You deserve someone better."

"Thanks."

"Someone that always stands by your side no matter what. Someone that puts you before himself, making sure you get home safe and you're always happy." He stared at her, waiting for her to say something. "A man who would die for you."

She said nothing for a long time. "Thank you, Henry."

His lips sagged in a frown as the silence dragged on between them. When she didn't say anything further, he lay down and turned on his side. "Good night."

She left the living room and disappeared into her bedroom. When she lay down in bed, she thought about Aaron. Their relationship was absolutely perfect. She had never been happier. But when he told her what he did, it completely turned her world upside down. It hurt more than anything. She had already experienced more pain than anyone should, but this burned like acid rain. She felt tricked. She trusted him more than anyone else, and he slid a knife in her back when she least expected it. It was a silent kill she didn't see coming. That's what made it worse.

She forced herself to get over him because she didn't want to be in pain anymore. They weren't getting back together so she couldn't think about him anymore, but she missed their physical relationship. She wanted to be with someone in the throes of passion. She could sleep with Aaron if she wanted to, but that wouldn't be fair to him or to her. She couldn't please herself the way she liked so she was sexually frustrated for half a year. It was killing her. She forced herself to count sheep so she could finally fall asleep.

The next morning, she donned her swimsuit and grabbed a towel before she crept into the living room. Henry was still asleep and she didn't want to wake him up. When she walked inside, he was already awake. He wore his swim trunks and a shirt.

He looked at her with a smile. "Going for a swim?"

"Why are you awake so early?"

He shrugged. "I rise when the sun does."

"You wanna come?"

"Of course." He rose to a stand then followed her out the door. When they walked down to the beach, he stripped off his shirt and revealed his naked chest. His chest was wide and his stomach was defined in muscles. Since Sydney was sexually frustrated, she looked away. Even if she wanted to sleep with Henry, she couldn't. She would never jeopardize their friendship or hurt him. She loved him. When she dropped her towel, he stared at her body

30

intently before he looked away. Sydney tried to act like she didn't notice.

She ran to the water and he followed right behind her. They swam through the ocean until their feet couldn't touch the bottom.

"How far do you want to go today?" he asked.

"Far," she said while she stayed afloat.

"You're crazy."

"You don't have to come."

"I wouldn't miss it."

She swam forward and he kept his pace alongside her. They swam out to the horizon, far away from the beach. They were even further out than the surfers.

"This is really dangerous," Henry said. "You shouldn't do this by yourself."

"I'm fine."

"What about sharks?"

"I'll take my chances," she said as she caught her breath.

"So why do you come out here?" he asked. "The view is the same as it is on the beach. And it looks better with a drink in your hand."

"Whales are migrating this time of year."

He raised an eyebrow. "Have you seen them before?"

"I've touched them."

"What? You've swam with whales?"

"It's the most amazing thing in the world."

"That isn't safe!"

She rolled her eyes. "I've never been safe."

"Well, I can change that."

"What?"

"Nothing," he said. "So how long do we wait?"

"As long as it takes."

"Well, let me know when you get tired."

Sydney peered into the water then dipped her ear down, waiting for the typical call of the whales. When she looked at Henry, he was staring at her, watching her every move.

"What happened yesterday?" she asked.

"What do you mean?"

"After school. We were talking about girls and you got all weird."

He looked away and stared at the shore for a moment. "Well, I—wasn't going to say anything but—"

"Did you hear that?"

"What?"

She dipped her head in the water again. "They're here."

Henry dipped under the water and started to look around. He came back up to the surface. "Holy shit! They're over there!" He pointed a few feet away. The dorsal fin of a blue whale protruded from the water.

She smiled. "Let's go!"

"What?"

"Come on." She gave his hand a squeeze then swam toward the whales.

Henry swam right after her.

Sydney dived under water and opened her eyes. It was dark so the only way she could see them was by their gigantic size. They moved through the water slowly. She kicked until she reached the side of a whale then ran her fingers across the skin. She saw Henry swim alongside her then hold onto the fin. A small calf was swimming alongside the mother and Sydney pointed at it. Henry nodded when he saw it too. When Sydney couldn't hold her breath any longer, she swam to the surface and gasped for air. Henry popped up a moment later.

"That was fucking awesome!" he said as he slammed his hand on the surface of the water.

She laughed. "I told you!"

He swam to her and wrapped his arm around her for a moment. "Thanks for showing me that."

She smiled. "You're welcome. There's nothing like it."

He stared at her face. "No, there isn't."

They both turned toward the whales and watched their fins glide in the water until they moved further out to sea. They said nothing for a long time.

"Well, I'm getting tired," Sydney said.

"Thank god. I was tired before the whales even came."

She laughed. "Let's go."

They swam back to shore then collapsed on the sand, lying side by side.

Henry tried to catch his breath. "That was too cool."

"Those whales are too cool."

"Sydney?"

"Henry?"

"Even though that was amazing, you really shouldn't do that alone. It isn't safe. Something could happen to you and no one would ever know."

She said nothing.

He sighed. "I know nothing I say will change your mind because you're unbelievably stubborn, but I mean it. Please think about it."

"Your words will be considered."

He rolled his eyes. "I admire your bravery and independence, but don't let it turn into pure stupidity."

"I can take care of myself, Henry." She rose from the sand then walked to her towel. After she dried herself off, she looked at him. He quickly looked away, acting like he hadn't just been staring at her.

He rose to a stand. "Now I'm starving."

"Me too."

"What are you making?"

"I'm too tired to cook. Let's go somewhere."

"Deal."

After they dried off, Sydney threw on a dress and Henry pulled on his shirt then they left for the Tiki Diner. When they walked inside, they both fell into a booth, exhausted.

The waitress came over and eyed their slumped shoulders and drooping eyes. "It's pretty early in the morning to be so tired."

Sydney smiled. "We were swimming with whales."

"Ooh. That sounds like fun."

"It was awesome," Henry said.

"What can I get you kids?"

"I'll have a waffle," Sydney said.

"The number three," Henry said as he handed her his menu. "And two coffees, please."

"Coming right up," she said as she walked away.

Henry stared at Sydney for a long time. "What do you want to do for the rest of the day?"

"Well, I have to call my mom and I have an— errand to run."

"An errand?"

"Yeah."

"Can I come?"

"Uh—no. It's personal."

He nodded. "Okay."

"What are you going to do for the day?"

"Check for posted grades every ten minutes."

She laughed. "I thought you wanted to enjoy your weekend."

"I just want to get it over with. If I got a C, I would be happy."

"I would pass out."

"Well, you shouldn't because it would obviously be a mistake."

"I don't know about that. I'm not as smart as everyone thinks."

The waitress brought their food and they ate in silence. Henry practically inhaled his breakfast while Sydney poked at her waffle.

"You aren't hungry?" he asked.

She was never hungry before she had to call her mother. It made her stomach turn inside out. "Not really."

"We just burned like ten thousand calories."

She smiled. "I know. I'll be hungry later."

He finished his plate clean then downed his whole mug of black coffee. When the waitress brought the check, Henry paid for the whole thing before Sydney could even grab her wallet.

"What was that?" she asked.

"What?"

"Why did you pay for everything? We always split the tab."

"What's the big deal? You can get mine later, right?"

"I guess."

"Now you can calm down," he said with a laugh. "Let's go."

Henry drove them back to the house. He turned off his car and walked Sydney to the door. She thought it was odd. He had never done that before.

"What are you doing?"

"What do you mean?"

"Why are you walking me to the door?"

He looked uncomfortable. "Uh—I left something inside."

"Oh, sorry." She opened the door and they both walked in. Henry grabbed his jeans and the shirt he was wearing the evening before.

"Well, I'll see you later."

"Bye, Henry."

"Bye." He walked out and shut the door behind him.

Sydney grabbed her phone and stared at it for a moment. The last thing she wanted to do was call her mom. She didn't hate her mom—she didn't like her, but she didn't necessarily hate her. Her stepfather was a different story.

She pressed the send button. "Hi, Mom," she said when she answered.

"Hello. How are you?"

"Good. You?"

"Good."

"How's school?"

"It's a lot of work but I'm learning a ton."

"And how's the aquarium?"

"Eh—I wish I wasn't a janitor, but I hope it leads to something else eventually."

"At least you have your foot in the door."

Sydney heard the loud sound of yelling in the background. "Is everything okay?"

"Uh, yeah. Dan is watching football."

Sydney knew football wasn't on Saturdays unless it was the playoffs. She didn't bother to tell her mom she caught her in a lie. What was the point? "So, what did you want to discuss?"

"Dan suggested that we go out there and spend Thanksgiving with you."

She felt her heart drop. She hadn't gone home once since she moved to Hawaii and she never planned to. She never expected them to come to her. "Uh, I don't think that's a good idea. I always have a lot of homework and I have to work on Thanksgiving."

"Well, we could still see you for a little bit. And Dan really wants to see the island."

"I guess you guys could stay at a hotel."

Sydney heard her stepfather in the background. "Did she say no?" The anger in his voice was unmistakable. "I already got the vacation time. You tell that bitch to do what she's told." She heard the phone being wrestled from her mother. "Did you just tell your mother no?" he snapped.

"No, sir," she said calmly, speaking like she was ordered to.

"You better. I'll smack that pretty little face off your head."

"Yes, sir," she responded automatically.

"We are coming for Thanksgiving and you're coming here for Christmas."

"What?"

"What did you say?"

"I'm coming there for Christmas?"

"You bet your ass you are. You keep up this lip and I'm gonna bloody it when I get there."

"Dan," she heard her mother say. Her stepfather must have smacked her mother because Sydney heard a whimper.

"We'll be there on Thanksgiving." He hung up.

Sydney dropped the phone on the ground and buried her face in her hands. The last thing she wanted to do was spend the holiday with her tormenter and her tormentor's son, who was just as terrifying. Before the tears could bubble up, she blinked them back and controlled her breathing. She wasn't going to cry about this. She was tired of crying. She only had to see them for a few days a year. As long as she kept her mind and her sanity, she would be okay. Her heart still palpitated in her chest in direct opposition to her thoughts.

She changed into her workout clothes then went to the gym. She had so much adrenaline pumping in her veins she thought she could punch her fist through solid steel.

When she walked inside, her trainer greeted her. "Hey, Sydney." He stared at her clenched jaw and her flexed hands. "Having a bad day?"

She walked down the hall and went into the private room, which was covered in mirrors on both sides and padding along the floor. "I've had better."

"Do you want to discuss it?"

"Not really."

"I still expect you to focus."

"That won't be a problem," she said as she tightened her thin gloves around her hands.

Jeremy, her trainer for the past two years, was someone she considered to be a friend but she couldn't talk about this with him—with anyone. She would take it to the grave. When they asked why she signed up for self-defense, kick boxing, marital arts, and street fighting, she always responded "recreational." There was nothing recreational about it. The only way she could sleep at night was because she knew she could break her stepfather's neck if she had to, along with that perverted son of his. They had tortured her long enough. If they made another move toward her and her mother did nothing to stop it, she would break their hand before they could even touch her. She was sick of the treatment. She thought she was safe living on an island but she wasn't. They were coming for her.

Jeremy started their sparring match by aiming a punch to her face. She blocked it and kicked his knees from under him. Before she could pin him to the ground, he tripped her then pushed her to the mat. She wrapped her legs around his neck and pulled him down. Then, she rose to her feet again. Like a snake and a crane, they moved across the floor, neither one gaining the advantage for long. They were both covered in sweat within a few minutes. Their skin was too slippery to grab onto.

Sydney laid the final strike when she kicked him then pinned his arms behind his back, bringing him to the floor. Jeremy was a big guy, easily twice her weight, and it made her smile knowing she could be his adversary. When they started years ago, she could barely block a single blow. It took them a long time to get to where they were now.

"Good job," he said, out of breath.

"Thanks," she said as she bent over.

"As much as I hate saying this, there's nothing more I can do for you. You're going to need to find another trainer."

"What? But I love working with you."

He smiled. "But in order to learn and grow, you need a new opponent and new teacher. I can train you and take your money for as long as you want, but I want the best for you. Whoever pissed you off has it coming. I definitely wouldn't want to be in a dark alley with you."

She laughed. "I don't know about that."

"I do. You can totally kick my ass."

"Well, I try."

"I'll give you a friend's number. He and a few guys work together. I'm sure you can find what you need there."

"Thanks." She walked over to him and hugged him. "Thanks for everything."

He patted her on the back. "Don't mention it. So now are you going to tell me who you intend to use this weapon on? An ex-boyfriend? A bully? The president of the United States?"

She smiled. "None of the above."

"Ex-girlfriend?"

"You wish."

"I'm not judging."

She was quiet for a moment. "My stepfather and my stepbrother."

He nodded. "I hope they get what's coming to them."

"Oh, they will."

"What did they do to you?"

She pulled her hair out of her face. "I'll take it to the grave."

## 5

"What does he want to talk about?' Henry asked as he walked beside Sydney and Nancy.

"Do you think you failed the exam?" Nancy asked.

"I don't know," Sydney said. "He just told me to meet him in his office."

They both looked at each other.

Sydney stared at them. "I'll tell you what he said as soon as I'm finished."

Henry met her gaze. "It's probably nothing. I doubt you failed the test or are being reprimanded for something. He probably wants to give you a basket of mini muffins because you're his favorite student ever."

"I hope so. And if I get some muffins, I'll share."

He smiled then hugged her. "You'll be fine."

When he pulled away, she realized they had been hugging a lot lately. That wasn't normal for them. She turned and walked down the hall, approaching the office. It was open when she reached it.

Professor Jones was leaning back in his chair, staring at his computer. When she walked inside, she noticed the human skull sitting on his filing cabinet. Football banners decorated the room along with a few pictures of his kids. One chair sat in front of the desk so she lowered herself into the seat.

"Hello, Dr. Jones."

He smiled. "Hello, Ms. Quartz. Thanks for stopping by."

"Did you want to discuss my exam?" She knew how nervous she sounded but she couldn't control her voice. A professor never called you in for good news—only bad.

"Well, no, but I guess that's relevant to this discussion. You got a perfect score—like usual."

She released the air from her lungs.

He laughed. "Were you worried?"

"I'm always worried."

"Well, you can calm down. I wanted to ask if you were interested in a tutoring position. I have a student in my class that requested one. Since you're at the top of the list, I decided to ask you first. It pays twenty dollars an hour."

She smiled. "Wow. I was not expecting that. Twenty bucks? I could use the cash."

"Great. I'll let him know. Could you start today?"

"When my classes are finished."

"That's perfect."

"Who's the student?"

He turned to his computer and searched for the name. "Let's see…here it is. Coen Marshall."

That caught her off guard. She knew he failed his exam but she never expected him to reach out for help. Perhaps she should have asked who the student was before she agreed. "Oh, okay."

"Is that a problem?"

Her cheeks flushed. "No. There's no problem."

"Okay. I'll tell him to meet you in the library at three."

"Thank you." She rose from the chair then left the office without saying goodbye, forgetting her manners completely. She didn't have a problem with Coen, hardly ever spoke to him, but she was attracted to him. She would just have to suck it up and be professional—and not think about kissing him. He was an asshole with a girlfriend anyway. She shouldn't want him. She shook her head and cleared her thoughts before she returned to her friends.

"What happened?" Nancy asked.

"He gave me a tutoring job."

"Oh, that's great," Henry said. "It's no muffins, but that's still good."

She nodded. "Yeah."

Henry immediately knew something was bothering her. "What's up?"

She shook her head. "Nothing."

"Who are you tutoring?" he asked.

"Coen."

Nancy's eyes widened. "Really? He actually requested a tutor. He seems like the type of guy who wouldn't care."

Henry was silent but his eyes were wide and his jaw tense.

"Well, apparently he does care," Sydney said.

"Did he personally request you?" Henry asked.

"I have no idea."

"Can you refuse the job?" he asked.

"She already agreed to it," Nancy said. "Besides, it's not a big deal. It's just Coen. He's not dangerous or anything."

"Are you sure you're okay with this?" Henry asked as he looked at her.

"Yeah. I don't know him very well—or at all—but we should be fine. It will probably only be an hour a day anyway."

Henry fell silent.

"Well, good luck with that," Nancy said with a smile. "I have to get to class."

"Bye," Sydney said.

Henry didn't watch her go. He was totally zoned out.

"You okay?" Sydney asked.

"What?"

"Are you okay?" she repeated.

"Yeah, yeah. Let's get to physio."

"Okay."

They went to their next class and sat in the back like they usually did. Henry didn't take notes again and she scribbled away on her notepad.

He leaned toward her and whispered, "I don't think he's a good guy."

"Coen?"

"Yeah."

"Okay." She didn't know what else to say.

"He was fighting with his girlfriend at the bonfire the whole time. That's all I ever see him do. Fight with chicks."

"Why are you telling me this?"

He shrugged. "Just in case you were wondering."

"I'm just tutoring him—that's it."

"So you aren't interested in him or anything?"

She shook her head. "He isn't my type."

"And what is your type?"

"I actually don't know."

He nodded and returned his attention to the front of the class. At the end of the period, they were given a quiz. Sydney scribbled her answers down while Henry left his blank. He obviously hadn't been paying attention for the entire period. She offered to let him copy but he refused the offer. Henry was always noble in that way. He wasn't a cheat or a liar. Sydney always liked that about him.

After class, they walked outside.

"I'll see you later," she said as she walked the opposite way to the library.

Henry walked beside her. "I can walk you."

"That's really unnecessary."

"I have to go to the bookstore anyway."

"For what?" she asked suspiciously.

"Scantrons."

"Oh."

They walked into the building together. When Sydney found Coen sitting in a study room, she stopped. "Well, thanks for walking me."

Coen looked up at them and watched them for a moment.

"Yeah." Henry wrapped his arms around her and held her for a long moment. Sydney returned his embrace awkwardly. He had already hugged her twice in one day. "Let me know if you want to do something later."

"Okay."

He turned around and walked away.

She took a deep breath before she walked into the room and shut the door behind her. "Hi," she said as she placed her backpack on the table.

"Hey," he said with a nod. His brown hair had slight curls at the end. It complemented his pale skin tone, which contrasted against the ridiculously blue color of his eyes. They were so bright she wanted to ask if he wore contacts. She knew she couldn't ask him that without getting yelled at or slapped. His t-shirt revealed the shape of his chest and torso. His shoulders were wide and so was his chest. His thin hips looked sexy on his small waist. When she glanced down to the floor, she saw his feet were in sandals. He even had nice toenails and feet. She liked it. When her thoughts turned lustful, his body on top of hers while he licked her everywhere, her screams of pleasure as he made her come, and her nails digging into his back, she immediately stopped them. She knew she needed to get laid soon. She hadn't had an orgasm in six months and it was really getting to her—*really getting to her*.

"So, I guess we can get started," she said awkwardly.

"Yeah."

Just him saying a simple word made her spine shiver. She hated herself for being shaken so easily. He was an asshole and a piece of shit boyfriend. She couldn't feel

45

attracted to him. Besides, she knew nothing would ever happen between them even if she wanted it to.

She pulled out her book and notepad and sat across from him.

"Shouldn't you sit next to me?" he asked.

"Wha—what? Why?"

"So I can see the textbook," he said with a raised eyebrow.

"Oh, of course. Yeah." She rose from her chair then sat beside him. When her arms brushed his, feeling the heat of his skin, she bit her lip. Sitting beside him was better than sitting across from him. Now she didn't have to look at his handsome face and could pretend he was a clown or something. "So what don't you understand?"

"Nothing."

She sighed. "Well, we can start from the beginning."

"No," he said. "I said I don't understand nothing, meaning that I understand everything."

She raised an eyebrow. "Are you trying to be a smart ass right now? Maybe you should change your degree to English."

He laughed. "No, I wasn't trying to be a dick. I just meant that I understand the material."

"Then why are you paying me to tutor you?"

"I'm not paying you—my father is."

"Well, why are you in need of my services at all?"

"Because I failed that test."

"I assumed so because it was blank."

"Why were you looking at my test?"

She stilled. "I just noticed when I walked by."

He stared at her. "When I failed that test, my dad called the professor and arranged a tutor. Since you're at the top of the class like a good little student, he picked you."

"So did you fail the exam on purpose?"

"No, I just couldn't concentrate."

"Why don't you ask to retake the exam?"

"Professor Jones said no."

"Why couldn't you concentrate?"

"It's personal."

She closed her books then leaned back in the chair. "Then what would you like me to do?"

He shrugged. "I can sit here and keep myself occupied and you can study. I'm sure that's what you would be doing anyway."

She crossed her arms over her chest. "It's very unethical for me to take your father's money without providing a service to you."

"Then don't take the money."

"Then don't make me stay here."

"I have to."

She sighed. "Well, we're here so why don't we study together?"

"I guess we can."

"Okay." She opened her notes and they reviewed the material together, testing each other as they went through the diagrams of specimens and their components. Sydney was really impressed by his knowledge of the material. He wasn't lying. He really did know his stuff.

When they had fifteen minutes left, Coen pushed the book away. "I'm done for the day."

"Me too."

"Are you named after the capital of Australia?" he asked suddenly.

"Are you named after the Cohen Brothers?"

He smiled. "I didn't ask to be rude. I'm sorry if my question offended you. But no, I'm not named after the Cohen Brothers, especially since we don't even spell our names in the same way."

She was quiet for a moment. "Yes."

"That's cool."

"Really?"

"I'm not making fun of you. I was just wondering."

"My family is from Australia. We moved to California when I was ten. My mom loved the city so much that she named me after it."

He nodded. "That's interesting. So how did you end up in Hawaii?"

"I wanted to go to college here. How did you end up here?"

"My family lives here. I'm a native."

She raised an eyebrow. "You don't look Hawaiian."

"I misspoke. I was born here."

"Oh. Cool."

"I couldn't imagine living anywhere else."

"Nor could I." She placed her books in her backpack then stood up. When she looked out the window of the study room, she saw Henry standing there, waiting for the tutoring session to end.

"Is that your boyfriend?" he asked. "He's very determined to claim his territory. I've never been silently threatened so much in my life."

"No," she said with a sigh. "He's not my boyfriend."

"Are you sure?"

She looked at him. "Yes, I'm sure."

"Well, you should tell him that. He clearly doesn't get it."

"He's just my friend. He probably has something to tell me."

"And a text wouldn't suffice?" He stood up and shouldered his pack. When he moved his arms, his shirt pressed tight against his body. She could see the lines of his muscles through the thin fabric. She was getting aroused just by looking at him. She hadn't been turned on like that in a really long time. Aaron didn't even make her that horny.

"You okay?"

"Huh?"

"I was talking and you totally zoned out on me."

"Sorry, I was thinking."

He raised an eyebrow. "Okay. Well, I have to get to work. Thank you for tutoring me."

"Yeah."

He opened the door and walked past Henry. Just like Coen said, Henry glared at him with pure hatred. Sydney was surprised by his obvious hostility. He clearly hated the guy.

Sydney stepped out of the room and looked at Henry. "Why are you here?"

"I had some trouble at the bookstore, and by the time I was done, your session was over. I just thought I would come by and see how it went."

She was still suspicious. "You couldn't wait until tomorrow?"

He averted his gaze. "I'm sorry. I didn't mean to upset you. I'll see you tomorrow." He turned to walk away but she grabbed him.

"Wait. You didn't upset me."

"I didn't?" he asked hopefully.

"I was just surprised to see you here. You were glaring at Coen like you hated him."

"Well, I think he's a jerk."

"You don't even know him."

"From what I've seen, I can tell he's a jerk. Plus, he has a tattoo."

"What's wrong with tattoos?"

He looked uncomfortable. "Nothing. I just get a bad vibe from him."

"He's actually really nice."

"He is?"

"At least he was to me."

Henry walked toward the door and she followed him. "Is he really stupid?"

"No. He's actually pretty smart. Since he failed that test, he has to be tutored."

"If he's smart, then why did he fail it?"

"He said he was distracted."

"By what?"

"He wouldn't say."

They walked to the parking lot until they reached their cars.

"Wanna go out to dinner?" he asked.

"I'm hitting the gym," she said.

"Oh, cool." He opened his car door. "I'll see you later then."

"Bye," she said as she waved. She climbed inside the Jeep and he waited for her to leave first, like he always did. Sydney pulled out of the parking lot then drove to the gym a few miles away. Jeremy had given her the number to a new fighting trainer and she made an appointment for that evening.

When she arrived, she walked into the locker room and changed into her tight-fitting spandex and her sports bra, the attire she was told to wear when training. The least amount of material would ensure that she was harder to grab and wouldn't get caught on anything. Also, it allowed the trainer to see her form as she moved.

After she was dressed, she walked to the front desk. "Hello. I have an appointed at four with a personal trainer."

The man looked at the computer. "Okay. I have you down here for workout room eight for the street fighting advanced level."

"Thank you," she said as she walked away.

When she reached the workout room, she placed her bag against the wall and stepped into the center of the studio, tightening her gloves around her wrists. The trainer was kneeled on the ground, working with the stereo. He had his shirt off. When she looked at the muscles in his back, another round of lust flooded through her. She shook her head. First, Coen and now she wanted to screw her trainer. She would have to get a vibrator or something otherwise she would start raping people.

When he stood and faced her, she felt her heart squeeze tightly, flushing the rest of her body with adrenaline. Her blood pounded in her ears and blocked out all other sound. Now she knew why she wanted to fuck her trainer—it was Coen.

He raised an eyebrow then looked at his clipboard. "I guess I should have looked at the name first. When Jeremy referred you, he spoke to someone else."

"Oh." She felt stupid for not saying something better.

He eyed her body, his look lingering on her breasts before he met her gaze. If she caught someone else looking at her like that, she would be pissed, but it was hot when Coen did it.

"Your paperwork says you're advanced, and Jeremy can't keep up with you anymore."

"I guess."

He stepped closer to her, and against her will, she looked down at his chest. He was perfectly sculpted. His chiseled eight pack tightened his waist, making him thin around the hips. His chest branched out into his wide shoulders. There were no blemishes or markings on his skin. He was perfect and beautiful. Her panties were already starting to soak. His best feature was his bright blue eyes. They reminded her of the depth of the ocean, full of life and mystery.

"What do you mean *you guess*?"

"What?"

He shook his head. "You seem more intelligent when we're in the classroom."

She was too turned on to respond to the insult.

"What is your interest in self-defense?"

"Protection," she said automatically.

"From what?"

"It's...personal."

"Your boyfriend can't protect you?"

"I don't have a boyfriend."

"He's in the relationship even if you aren't."

"What?"

"I guess you're only book smart, not common sense smart."

"Excuse me?"

"Your friend is in love with you. Or did you not notice?"

"No, he isn't," she said quickly. "He's just my friend."

He shook his head. "You are totally ignorant to what goes on around you, you can't answer a question most of the time, and you zone out randomly."

"You've just caught me on a bad day."

"I guess we'll find out."

"So you're a trainer?"

He raised an eyebrow. "You just figured that out?"

She sighed. She knew how stupid she sounded. "Since when?"

"A couple years ago. I have three black belts and I've mastered jiu jitsu, kick boxing, and street fighting. You really don't want to piss me off. And you didn't answer my question. Why do you want to learn self-defense?"

"I said it was personal."

"That isn't good enough for me. How am I supposed to give you the results you want if I don't know what your goal is?"

She was quiet for a moment. "I just want to be able to fight against two men at once."

He raised an eyebrow. "That's very specific."

"Well, you asked."

"Are you in danger?"

"You tell me."

"Don't be a smart ass." He stepped close to her and pressed his face against hers. "Is someone threatening to hurt you?"

She wanted to tell Coen the truth but she couldn't. She was surprised that she even considered it at all. "No."

"You aren't a very good liar."

She averted her gaze.

"Look at me when I talk to you."

"You were a lot nicer an hour ago."

"When we're in this room, don't ever expect me to be nice to you. That's not what you're paying me to do," he said as he stepped back. "So are you going to tell me the truth?"

"No."

"Fine." He turned on the music. "Let's get started." He tossed the remote on the ground then rushed her, tripping her to the floor. After she felt his body on top of her, she had absolutely no desire to get him off. Her first thought was to wrap her legs around his waist and ask him to fuck her, but logic finally returned.

She rolled him off and tried to pin him to the floor but he threw her off. When he rushed her again, she dodged his body then landed a punch on his mouth. He returned with his own strike but missed when she ducked.

Sydney concentrated and avoided most of his hits then returned with her own strikes. She was fast, but he was equally quick with more strength. He had a look of anger on his face the entire time. She liked the expression. Everything about him turned her on. After twenty minutes of sparring, neither one having the upper hand, she let him tackle her to the floor. When he tried to pin her down, she made a weak attempt to move. His face was close to hers and she felt his heavy chest push against her breasts. Their breathing was both quick and heavy. A drop of his sweat fell on her neck and she liked it. His hips were pressed against hers, and after a second, she felt the bulge in his crotch form. She could tell how big he was and that just made her more frustrated with longing for him. Coen wasn't ashamed of having a boner on top of her. It was obvious that she felt it. How could she not?

"Aren't you going to try to get away?"

She just lay there, breathing heavily. The last thing she wanted to do was run. She had to mentally stop herself from kissing him, feeling his lips against her own. She had never been attracted to someone like that other than Aaron. Why did she only like assholes? Henry was a great guy. Why couldn't she like him?

He finally got off her. She wanted to scream.

"That ends this session." He stood up and grabbed her hand, pulling her to a stand. "Your form and timing are good. You're quick on your feet, but you lack initiative. You tried to avoid my attacks but rarely made any of your own. If you want to run from someone, then keep it up. If you want to defeat them, this behavior will have to change."

"Okay," she said with a nod.

"Overall, I was impressed. I wasn't expecting you to be so strong."

She tucked her hair behind her ear. "Thanks."

"I wish you would tell me who is responsible for this."

She said nothing.

He leaned toward her lips. "I'll make you tell me eventually."

She breathed in his scent, the mixture of sweat and blood, pure masculinity, and wanted to taste it on her lips. She was speechless, overcome by her desire.

He walked away then turned off the stereo. He grabbed his shirt then pulled it over his head, hiding the rest of this body. Now she understood why his girlfriend was willing to forgive him for cheating on her. He was a hot piece of ass. She shook her head. She had to stop thinking about that.

Coen walked to the door then held it open for her. Coen escorted her from the lobby to the parking lot.

"Same time tomorrow?" he asked.

"Uh, I only train three days a week."

"I meant for tutoring."

"Oh, yeah."

"Cool." He got inside his car and drove away. She climbed up into her Jeep and sat inside, relieved that he was finally gone. All she could think about was sex when she was around him. Now she wasn't sure if she was just insanely horny or if Coen was responsible for her lust.

When she got home, she showered then went straight to bed, exhausted by the long day. She wanted to fall asleep so she could stop thinking about Coen, wondering what he looked like naked and how big his cock was.

When she started to dream, she fantasized about Coen. They were fucking all over the house, in her bed, in the shower, on the beach—everywhere. Sweat covered her body as she explored the realms of her passion during her unconscious state. His body was on top of hers, his wide chest completely dominating her, and he was moving deep inside her with her legs pinned back while she begged him to fuck her harder.

She came harder than she ever had before, screaming incoherently. The sound of her moans woke her up. She sat up in bed, recovering from the blissful orgasm. She was out of breath and soaked in sweat. Her underwear were drenched and the sheets were wet. It was the first time she'd come in six months and she wanted to do it again. She went back to sleep as quickly as she could.

# 6

She went to work a few hours before her first class. A few of the tanks needed to be cleaned and the plants needed to be trimmed in some sections of the wildlife preservation. She didn't mind getting up early to go to work. Even though she was just cleaning, she loved being with the marine wildlife.

When she was finished for the day, she was walking out when she ran into Dr. Goldstein, one of the leading scientists of the aquarium.

"Hello, Dr. Goldstein," she said with a smile.

"Hello, Stacy." He nodded.

"It's Sydney, actually."

"Well, have a good day," he said as he continued on his way.

She sighed. She had been trying to get in his good graces for months. She even cleaned his lab and the equipment in it, hoping he would notice her. He was leading an exhibition out to sea to study great white sharks, and she really, really wanted to be a part of it. She couldn't just ask him for an invitation so she had to get under his radar.

She ran into Henry in the parking lot.

"Good morning," he said with a yawn.

"Hey," she said awkwardly. After the dream she had about Coen, she felt awkward around Henry and guilty about the raw sexual feelings she had for Coen. She also wondered if he really did have feelings for her. Coen said he did, but he didn't even know Henry. "I saw Dr. Goldstein."

"How'd that go?"

"Keeps calling me Stacy."

He cringed. "Sorry. It doesn't sound like you're getting anywhere."

"No, not at all."

"Keep trying."

"I've been trying for months. That field mission will be launched soon."

"Maybe he would notice you more if you weren't wearing that baggy jumpsuit. No one looks attractive in that."

"I don't want him to notice me because of my appearance, Henry."

"Well, if you're desperate, you have to do everything you can, right?"

"I suppose."

They got inside their cars and drove to the campus. Every song on the radio reminded her of Coen so she shut it off. But she kept thinking about him, especially in sexual ways. She had to see him in her next class and wasn't sure what she was supposed to do. Should she say hi to him? Ignore him? Act like nothing had changed? She knew she would blush when she looked at him, especially after all the nasty shit he did to her last night in her sleep. She hadn't had an orgasm like that ever—not even with Aaron. She had to change her underwear twice.

When they got to the building, they walked to their zoology class and sat down. Coen was already sitting to the left and one row ahead. He didn't look at her or acknowledge her in any way. She wasn't sure if she should feel upset, hurt, or relieved by his complete indifference. She tried to focus on the lecture as the period went by. When the class was over, she went back to thinking about Coen.

When they walked to their next class, Nancy looked at Sydney. "So how did it go with him?"

"It was fine," Sydney said with a smile.

"Why are you smiling?" Nancy teased.

"No reason," she said quickly.

Henry looked at her then turned away, obviously displeased by the look.

"What's he like?" Nancy asked.

"He's actually really nice and very smart."

"Then why does he need a tutor?"

She sighed. "It's personal." Sydney and Henry left Nancy then went to their physio class. She started to concentrate on the powerpoint but Coen came back into her mind, and of course, he was naked. She kept forcing herself to concentrate on the lecture but images of them having sex flooded her brain. She knew it needed to stop. He had a girlfriend and he was a heartbreaker.

When her classes were over, she felt her heart fall. Now she had to tutor Coen. She was excited to see him, but equally frightened. When she left the building, Henry was supposed to walk to the parking lot but he followed her instead.

"Where are you going?" she asked.

"I'm walking with you to the library."

"Why?"

He shrugged. "I don't have anything else to do. I don't work today."

"Henry, I don't need you to walk me anywhere."

"I don't mind."

"Well, I do. And please don't pick me up either."

He stared at her for a moment. "I didn't mean to offend you."

He was such a sweet guy that it was hard for her to stay angry with him. "You didn't. I just don't need a friend to walk me everywhere."

"Do you not want Coen to see you with anybody?"

"What? What does that mean?"

"Nothing," he said quickly.

"I'll see you later."

"Can I see you tonight?"

"Um, I think so. I'll text you."

He smiled. "Okay. I look forward to it."

"Bye," she said as she walked toward the library. After she entered the building, she felt her heart accelerate as she moved up the stairs. When she walked down the hall, she saw him sitting in the study room, looking at his phone. She took a deep breath before she walked in.

"Hey," she said as she sat down next to him.

"You sore?"

She flinched. "What? Why?" Did he know?

He raised an eyebrow. "We pushed it pretty hard yesterday. I thought you might be a little uncomfortable."

"Oh."

"What did you think I meant?"

"Nothing."

"Fine. Keep your secrets."

She looked away and opened the book.

"So, are you going to answer me?"

"Answer what?"

"How do you always get the highest grade in the class when you don't remember anything I say?"

She stared at him blankly.

He leaned forward. "Are you sore?"

"Oh," she said with a small laugh. "No. I work out all the time."

"What else do you do?"

"I swim."

"At the gym?"

"In the ocean. I swam with whales the other day."

His eyes widened. "You swim that far?"

"I guess."

"*You guess?*"

"Yes, I swim far," she answered.

"You're odd."

"No. You are."

"Me?"

"Yeah," she snapped. "You always ask me a million questions."

"I wouldn't have to ask you a million questions if you just answered my question instead of making me repeat it a million times."

"You're such a smartass."

"What's your point? You sound blonde most of the time."

"I do not."

"If only you can hear yourself talk."

"I'm just nervous."

He was quiet for a moment. "I make you nervous?"

"No," she said quickly. "I've never tutored someone before. It makes me nervous."

"Well, don't be."

"You make it sound so easy."

He leaned back in his chair then looked through the glass of the study room. "Your boyfriend didn't walk you here today?"

"He's not my boyfriend. I've said that at least ten times."

"Then why are you always together?"

"You've seen me with him once."

"You have every class together and you always sit by each other. I saw you with him at the bonfire, and I know he stays at your place a lot."

She raised an eyebrow. "How do you know all of that?"

"Word gets around."

"Well, he's not my boyfriend. Nothing is going on between us."

"You swear?"

"What does it matter?"

"Answer me."

The command in his voice made her shiver. "I swear."

"Is he gay?"

"No."

"Then what do you guys do together all the time?"

"Go swimming, watch television, work together, just normal stuff."

"That guy is insanely in love with you."

"You just asked if he was gay."

"I just had to make sure. But he's totally infatuated with you. Please tell me you notice it."

"No. If he had feelings for me, I would know by now."

"Ask him."

"What? No. That would make things awkward."

"Only if he answered yes."

"I'm not going to ask him that."

"Because you know he does."

"No, he doesn't."

"Yes, he does."

She felt her anger bubble to the surface. "How's your girlfriend? You like getting slapped by her?"

His smile dropped. "I don't have a girlfriend."

"Liar."

"What did you just say to me?"

"I said you're a liar."

"I'm not a liar," he said as he leaned toward her. "I don't have a girlfriend."

"Then what was that show on the beach?"

"Me trying to get her to leave me alone. We broke up months ago but she won't let me go."

"Sure."

"What's your problem? If you have something to say to me, just say it." Sydney said nothing. "I don't have a girlfriend and I haven't had one in four months."

She opened the book and flipped through the pages. "Let's start on the different phyla."

He shut the book. "Look at me."

She took a deep breath then faced him. "Why do you care what I think?"

"You're my friend—that's why."

"I am?"

"I thought so. Maybe I'm wrong."

She played with the edge of the book for a moment. "I want to be your friend."

"Friends trust each other. I said I don't have girlfriend—I'm not lying."

"Then why don't you believe me when I say I'm not with Henry?"

"I do believe you, but I know he has feelings for you. You should be careful."

"Be careful?"

"You love him, right? As your friend?"

"He's family to me."

"Then you need to be careful. Don't break his heart and lead him on."

"How am I leading him on?"

"You spend a lot of time with him and you let him hug you all the time. Girlfriends don't even hug each other that much."

She looked out the window, not willing to meet his gaze.

"I don't know why you're in denial about this. You're amazing. Of course the guy is going to fall in love with you."

She looked at him, raising an eyebrow. "I thought you said I was stupid?"

"I said you sound stupid."

"That isn't much better."

He smiled. "I guess not. I take it back."

"Thank you."

"But I know I'm right about Henry. If you love the guy, you should either talk to him or make it clear that you have no interest in him."

"And how would I do that?"

He shrugged. "Get a boyfriend." He stared at her for a long time, looking into her eyes.

"Well, I don't have anyone in mind."

"Nobody? Not a single person?"

She avoided his look. "No."

"I find that hard to believe."

"Who are you interested in?"

"Me?"

"Yeah, you. You're single. Who's on your radar?"

He shrugged. "I can't think of any names at the moment."

"Just bra sizes?"

He glared at her. "Why do you think I'm a pig?"

"Because you are."

"You just met me. How could you possibly know if I am or not."

"I've heard things about you."

He sighed. "I thought you were different."

"What?"

"You believe the 'things' you hear from random places? I thought you were a scientist? Look for the facts before you make a hypothesis, and only then is it an educated guess. It'll take more time and thought before it's a theory."

She was quiet for a moment. "I apologize."

"Thank you."

"So are you a pig?"

"I don't know. How do you define a pig?"

"Someone who sleeps around, never loves anyone and only wants to get laid. They only care about themselves. They lie, cheat, and steal to get what they want."

He nodded. "Well, I kinda am a pig, then."

She stared at him, waiting for him to elaborate.

"I've slept around, but I've loved someone with my whole heart, and I care more about that than fucking a random list of women. I've never lied, cheated, or stolen. The women I've fucked knew that's exactly what I wanted from them, nothing more."

She opened the book and flipped through the pages, picking up where she left off.

"No response?"

"What do you want me to say?"

"Do you think I'm a pig?"

"I don't know."

"The answer is pretty clear."

"It is?"

"I'm not."

She ignored his comment. "We should get to work."

He looked at the clock. "Our session is over."

"Is it?" She looked at the time. "Wow."

"Time flies when you're having fun, right?"

"I guess."

"Let's go out for some juice."

"What?"

"The kind that's squeezed from fruit. They make smoothies out of it, like Jamba Juice?"

"You want to go do something?"

"Yeah. It will be fun. Let's go."

"Uh." She tried to grasp the next words to say.

He grabbed her arm and pulled her to stand. "Let's head out."

Once she was on her feet, she grabbed her backpack from the table. When they left the library, she felt her heart hammer in her chest. Was this a date? What the hell just happened? Did he like her? If he did, she knew she shouldn't get involved with him. He would just break her heart and rip it into pieces like Aaron did. "Actually, I have plans tonight."

"What plans?" he asked while looking into her face.

64

"My friends and I—"

"You're a horrible liar."

"I'm not lying."

He laughed. "You're just making it worse."

Her face turned red.

When they reached the parking lot, he walked to his Tacoma and opened the passenger door for her. She eyed it suspiciously.

"I told you I'm not a pig."

She got inside and he shut the door behind her.

When he got into the driver's seat, he leaned toward her. "You can calm down. We're just hanging out." He cranked the engine then pulled out of the driveway.

Her heart was racing in her chest as they drove down the highway to the other side of the mountain peaks. She assumed they were going to the tourist spot with a lot of restaurants and bars. When he pulled over, she saw the ocean on the left hand side. She never grew tired of watching it.

"And that's why I'll never move," he said as he looked out her window.

"It's beautiful."

He got out and opened the door for her. After he shut it, they walked to the juice stand that faced the beach.

"What would you like?" he asked.

"Pineapple."

"That's what I'm going to get too."

He paid for the drinks then they walked down to the beach.

"Why did you want to get juice?" she asked as she sat down.

"I assumed you didn't care for alcohol."

"What makes you think that?"

He shrugged. "You just don't seem like it."

She sipped her drink and looked straight ahead. A few people were walking their dogs along the sand. A group of tourists took pictures of the ocean from every angle. It was a waste of film. Something as beautiful as the Hawaiian shoreline could only be appreciated in real life.

"So, why do you need to learn self-defense?"

She raised an eyebrow. "Is that what this is all about? Interrogating me?"

"Maybe. Why won't you just tell me?"

"It's personal."

"You already said that. Tell me the truth."

"Please drop it."

"Answer me this."

"What?"

"Does Henry know?"

"No."

"So no one knows?"

"No."

"You're going to take it to your grave?"

"Yes."

He shook his head. "I'm asking as your instructor. Maybe I can help you."

"I don't need your help. I can take care of myself."

"I believe that. But I also believe having help will only make it easier."

She looked at him. "Coen, please drop it. I won't ask you again."

He met her gaze with the blue color of his eyes, which were sparkling bright. Every time she looked at him, she wanted to kiss his lips. She glanced at them then looked away. His shoulders were broad and wide and she wanted to rub her hands over them. This unstoppable attraction was starting to drive her insane. She accused him of being a pig but perhaps she was the pig. All she could think about was having sex in the back of his car.

"What are you thinking about?"

She flinched. "Uh...work."

"Why are you thinking about that?"

66

She tried to think of something to say. "There's this researcher that's about to take his work into the field. I've been trying to get his attention but he can't even remember my name."

"Where do you work?"

"The aquarium."

"Who is this guy?"

"Dr. Goldstein."

He nodded. "And why do you want to do research with him?"

"I want to be a marine biologist. He's published over twenty papers in his career. It's astonishing. I've cleaned his lab and equipment, talked to him about his work, but he keeps calling me Stacy."

"Don't take it personally," he said.

"I try not to."

They were both quiet. Coen drank his juice then put down the empty cup.

"Can I ask you something, Coen?"

"Yeah."

"What's your girlfriend's name?"

His eyes shined with anger. "I don't have a girlfriend."

"Sorry," she said quickly. "I mean your ex-girlfriend. The one from the bonfire."

He sighed. "Audrey."

"And what happened with her?"

He looked away. "I'll tell you when you tell me why you want to learn self-defense."

"I guess I'll never find out, then."

"I guess not."

"Did you love her?"

"I thought I did."

She nodded. "I'm sorry it didn't work out."

He didn't respond to her comment. "Why did you and Aaron break up?"

She raised an eyebrow. "How do you know about him?"

"College isn't much different than high school."

She sighed. "He cheated on me."

"I'm sorry."

"Yeah."

"Did you love him?"

"Yeah."

"Do you still?"

"I guess."

"So you aren't over him?"

"No, I am. But a part of me will always care about him in a different way than everyone else."

"Well, that fucker sounds like an idiot. I don't like him."

She smiled. "Neither do my friends."

"I bet Henry despises him."

"He isn't his biggest fan."

"Have you been with anyone since?"

"No, I haven't been dating."

"You aren't ready to move on?"

"No. I just haven't found anyone that I liked."

"Have you been fucking anyone?"

"That's a personal question."

"I didn't mean to offend you. You don't have to answer that."

"No."

"No, what?"

"I haven't been with anyone else." She wasn't sure why she told him that. It just came out.

"I've fooled around with a few girls. They were all hit and runs."

"How can you do that?"

"It's just the physical act. No love is involved."

"I could never do that."

"You fucked Aaron."

"That's different."

"How?"

"I love him."

"So you never fucked? You just made love the whole time?"

"No, I didn't say that."

"Then you have fucked just to fuck."

"I've never screwed someone outside of a relationship."

"You've never met someone that you just wanted to be physical with? You didn't want a relationship but you definitely wanted that?"

She felt her cheeks blush so she looked away. That was exactly how she felt for Coen. "No."

He smiled. "I know when you're lying. You may as well drop the act."

She dug her toes in the sand, feeling the grains touch her skin.

"You're denying yourself satisfaction by being a prude like that."

"I'm okay."

"When's the last time you had sex?"

"We just became friends and now you think you can ask me whatever you want?"

"I know you'll answer. So when?"

"Six months ago."

"Yikes. That's—wow."

"It's been hard."

"I bet it has," he said with a laugh. "You must miss it."

"I guess."

"Well, that wasn't a lie but it wasn't true either."

"Okay. I miss it a lot."

"Well, you're gorgeous. You could have your pick of any guy you want."

"You think I'm gorgeous?"

"I definitely think that. I'm surprised you don't."

Her cheeks blushed.

"I'm available if you need my services."

"Excuse me?"

"I'm just saying," he said with a laugh. "If you need help in that department, I wouldn't mind stepping up."

"And what makes you think I would even be interested?"

"You are on a date with me, aren't you?"

"You said we're just hanging out."

"On a date," he said with a smile.

There was a tingling sensation in her fingertips and her toes. She was insanely attracted to Coen and he would sleep with her if she asked him to, but she knew she couldn't do it. She would fall for him and he would just leave, breaking her heart. He wanted her to be someone that he just fucked—never made love to.

She hugged her knees to her chest then looked out at the water. "I think I'm ready to go now."

He was quiet for a moment. "Okay." He stood up then pulled her to her feet. They walked back to the car and he helped her get in the passenger seat. "I hope I didn't make you uncomfortable, Sydney," he said as he looked at the road straight ahead.

She stared out the window, seeing he sun set behind the horizon.

"I like you. I want to spend more time with you—more dates."

"I—I don't know."

"I know you like me."

"What makes you think that?"

"You're nervous around me—really nervous. I hear you talk to your friends and teachers. You're only this way around me. I make you nervous and excited at the same time. I give you butterflies."

She looked out the window, hiding her face. She wished she hadn't been so obvious.

When he pulled into the parking lot, he parked next to her car. "Thanks for getting juice with me."

"Yeah. Thanks for taking me."

"Have a good night."

She nodded then opened the door, relieved that he dropped the serious conversation. She got out of his car her then hopped inside her own. He stayed beside her while he waited for her to start her car. Every time she cranked the engine, it wouldn't start. She took the key out and inserted it again, but it still wouldn't go. The Jeep wasn't that old. She really didn't want to buy a new one.

"Car trouble?" he asked as he got out.

She cranked it again. "It won't start."

"Take the key out. You'll flood it with gas." He opened the hood and looked inside for a while. When he closed the engine, he wiped his hands on his jeans. "I don't know what the problem is. I'll have my uncle come look at it tomorrow. He's a mechanic."

"I'll just call my insurance."

"No," he said quickly. "He'll do it for free."

"Are you sure?"

"Yeah. Don't worry about it."

She was touched that he was willing to help her so much.

"Let me take you home." He was standing at her side.

"It's okay. I can call a friend."

"Get in," he said as he opened the passenger door of his car.

She sighed then did as he commanded.

"Good girl," he said as he closed the door.

After he got inside the car, he drove them out to the road. She gave him directions on how to get to her secluded house by the beach. When he pulled into the dirt driveway under the trees, he gasped.

"Wow. This place is awesome."

"Thanks," she said with a smile.

"You live on the beach?"

"Pretty close to it."

"How did you get this place? Do you have roommates?"

"I inherited it."

He got quiet. "Oh. I'm sorry."

"Thank you."

He opened the door then got out. She followed him to the front door. She wasn't sure if he was planning on walking her to the door or coming in. She didn't know how she felt about either option.

When they walked up the steps, she grabbed her keys from her bag. "Thank you for taking me home."

"Of course." He put his hands in his pockets and looked at her. She knew she should look away. His lips looked too sexy. She wanted to kiss him even though she shouldn't. She looked at the keys in her hand.

"Can I come inside?" he asked. "I would like to see your place."

She felt her hands start to sweat. She didn't trust herself to be alone with him. They would somehow end up naked on her bed, fucking like animals. Or at least that's what she wanted to do. She assumed he did as well.

"I'm not going to be a pig, if that's what you're worried about."

She smiled. "You'll be a gentleman?"

"Yes."

"Okay." She unlocked the door and they walked inside. She set her bag down like she did every day and walked into the living room. Coen moved around and looked at all the furniture and pictures on the tables. He went to the back door and looked at the view of the ocean.

"This place is just too good to be true."

"Yeah, I love it."

"You should."

"It's perfect. It's small but I don't need more than this."

"I agree." He came back to her and looked at her. "Can I stay awhile?"

"Sure. Are you hungry?"

"That depends. Are you a good cook?"

"I know a thing or two."

"Then yes, I'm hungry."

She turned around and started pulling ingredients together. He took a seat at the kitchen table and watched her but said nothing. She cooked rice with chicken then sliced some vegetables on the counter. She felt him watching her and it made her nervous.

"Do you pay rent?" he asked.

"No. It's paid off."

"So why do you work?"

"Food, gas, phone bill."

"That's nice."

"Yeah. I don't have any complaints." Her phone started to buzz on the counter. She didn't touch it because her hands were wet and sticky, but she looked at the screen. It was Henry. She remembered that she was supposed to call him.

"Let me guess who it is," he said with a smile. "Shakespeare wrote a play about him?"

She ignored him.

"You should tell him about us soon."

"Us?" she asked as she washed her hands in the sink. "There's nothing to tell."

"Yeah, there is. You and I are dating."

"No, we aren't."

"Yes, we are."

"I just met you."

"What's your point?"

She walked over and stopped in front of him. "I don't know what impression I—"

He pulled her into his lap, her face an inch away from his. She was silent as she felt his hands on her hips. He rubbed his nose against hers and stared into her eyes, making her heart melt. She was speechless, unable to say anything.

She stared at his lips. "I thought—you were going to be a—gentleman?"

"Do you want me to be?" he whispered.

"I—I don't know."

He pressed his forehead against hers. "I'll play it safe since you're unsure."

"Uh, okay."

He kissed the tip of her nose. "I really like you, Sydney."

"You don't even know me," she whispered. "I'm not the kind of girl you want."

"And what kind of girl do I want?"

"Someone that sleeps around. I'm not like that."

"I'm glad you aren't like that."

"What?"

"I want to get to know you better. I respect you."

She placed her hands on his shoulders. "No. I can't."

"Can't what?"

"I don't trust you."

"Why not? I won't lie to you, Syd."

"You're just going to get me into bed then never call me again. Make me fall in love with you before you disappear. Then, you are going to cheat on me. I can't deal with that a second time."

"I'm not going to do any of those things."

"You're right. You're not." She rose from the chair then stepped away from him. "I think you should go. I don't want you here." She hid her face from him so he couldn't see her vulnerability.

"No."

"I just asked you to leave."

"If I leave, you'll avoid me and I'll never get a chance to convince you that I'm not going to hurt you."

"Words are only words."

He came up behind her and wrapped his hands around her waist, pulling her against his chest. "Listen to me. I really like you, Syd. And I want a chance to be with you. We can take this as slow as you want." She tried to move from his arms but he kept her there, against his beating heart. "Let's start dating. We won't have sex and I won't cheat on you. We don't have to do anything if you don't want to. Just spend more time with me."

She turned around and looked at him. "I said no."

"And I don't accept that answer." He pressed his forehead against hers. "I won't have sex with you even if you beg me to."

"What makes you think I would even want to?"

He smiled. "You aren't fooling anybody."

She blushed, ashamed that he recognized the desire in between her legs.

"Just date me. I won't see anyone else and I won't lie to you. Spend more time with me, please."

"We can try."

He smiled. "Thank you." He kissed her on the forehead. "That's all I want."

She wrapped her arms around his neck and held him close to her. Feeling his strong body was arousing and relaxing at the same time. She had a feeling she would regret it, but she wanted him so much that she couldn't stop herself.

"Finish dinner," he whispered.

"Okay." She turned away then finished the remaining touches of the meal. She placed the food on the table then sat down. She was about to grab her fork when there was a knock on the door.

"I'll be right back," she said.

"Okay."

She walked to the front door then opened it. "Henry?"

"Hey," he said with a sigh. "I was worried. You didn't return my calls." He looked over his shoulder at Coen's car. "And whose car is that? What happened to yours?"

"Well, my car wouldn't start in the parking lot so Coen gave me a ride home."

He was quiet for a moment. "Is he still here?"

"Uh, yeah."

"Is he leaving now?"

"Um, no. I made dinner. He wanted to see the house."

He had a pained expression on his face. The light in his eyes was absent and he didn't meet her gaze. He stared at the door frame instead of Sydney. Now she felt so stupid for not seeing it before. Henry did have feelings for her. "Are you—on a date?" he whispered.

She couldn't stand the pain in his eyes. It was heartbreaking. "No," she lied.

He breathed a sigh of relief. "Oh, okay."

She stepped toward him and wrapped her arms around his shoulders, trying to hide her face from view. He wrapped his arms around her waist and held her close to him, breathing in her scent. They stood there together for a long time. When she thought she had her emotions under control, she pulled away. "I'll see you tomorrow, okay?" she said with a fake smile.

"Okay. Let me know if you want me to get rid of him."

She nodded. "I'm fine. But, thanks."

"Bye," he said as he walked back to his car.

After Sydney closed the door, she slid to the floor and hugged herself. Tears fell from her eyes now that she saw the truth of Henry's affection. He was totally and completely in love with her. Why hadn't she seen it before?

Coen walked into the room and sat on the ground across from her. He didn't say anything but nothing needed to be said.

She reached her hands out, beckoning him to her. He leaned against the wall and wrapped his arms around her. She turned into his shoulder and rested her face against his chest.

He stroked her hair. "I'm sorry."

## 7

"I didn't want to be right, you know."

She nodded. "I know." She stared at her hands, looking at their shape and texture. She was trying to get her mind off the harsh reality. "I can't hurt him. I love him so much. I can't do it."

He lifted her up and carried her to the couch. "I know."

"What am I going to do?"

"Tell him the truth."

"It'll kill him."

"Well, what did he think when he saw my car in the driveway?"

"That we were on a date."

"And he was okay with that?"

"I lied and said we weren't."

He nodded but didn't say anymore.

"When he thought we were more than friends, he looked like the world had ended. I couldn't tell him the truth—not like that."

"Then what are you going to do?"

"I have no fucking idea. I want to cause him the least amount of pain as possible."

He sighed. "You're going to cause him pain no matter what you do."

"I know."

"Sit down and talk to him. Tell him that you don't have feelings for him but you love him more like a brother. Then, tell him about me."

"I'm not going to tell him about you."

He raised an eyebrow. "So you're just going to lie to him? You know how shitty he's going to feel when he hears it from everyone else?"

"We won't tell anyone else."

"What? We are just going to keep everything a secret?"

"Yes."

"I didn't agree to that."

"Well, I'm not gonna drop a bomb like that on him. If I talk to him, I need to give him time to accept what I say before he sees me with someone else. I'm not cruel, Coen."

"Well, I don't like being someone's dirty secret."

"It wouldn't be like that."

"That's how I feel."

"You asked me if I wanted to start dating—not be in a committed relationship."

"Yes, but I didn't say I wanted it to be a secret. I want to take you out to ice cream, the movies, the beach—public places."

"I know this isn't fair to you, but we either keep it secret for a while or this isn't going to happen. I love Henry. I need to make sure he's okay first."

"I'm not trying to be cold, but his feelings aren't your problem. He's a man—he'll get over it."

"I realize that but I don't want to lose what we have. He's my best friend. I don't want him to disappear from my life because I didn't handle this right."

"That's a very likely scenario no matter what you do. I'm sure he's had feelings for you the entire time you've been friends, so in a way, you've never been friends. He's wanted to get with you the entire time. He probably wouldn't spend so much time with you if he wasn't in love with you. And to get over you, he's going to want space. He can't see you every day and not feel that way."

She ran her fingers through her hair. "You aren't making me feel better."

"I'm not trying to."

"What do I do? What do I do?" She leaned back on the couch and crossed her arms over her chest.

"Have him come over tomorrow and tell him the truth. That's step one."

"What's step two?"

"You won't know until you see how he reacts."

"I'm not telling him about you."

He sighed. "Fine. But I'm not going to stay in the closet forever. I'm giving you a small amount of time."

"Thanks for being so understanding," she said sarcastically.

"You're lucky I'm putting up with it at all. I hate lying and being deceitful."

"Well, I'll tell him tomorrow after school."

"Maybe we can set him up with someone. I have a few girl friends."

"Henry is very attractive. I'm sure he can get his own dates if he wants them."

He leaned back on the couch and placed his hand on mine. "It'll be okay."

She smiled. "Thanks for trying to make me feel better."

"Don't get used to it," he teased. "Can we stop talking about Henry now?"

"Yeah."

"Good. Because I want to invite you to dinner tomorrow night."

She wished she had the strength to say no, but she was weak. Coen made her feel weak, excited, and crazy all at the same time. "Okay."

He smiled. "I thought I would have to convince you."

"I thought so too."

"I'll pick you up at seven."

"Okay."

He stared at her for a long time, his blue eyes shining bright. Waves of passion vibrated in his eyes. She felt unnerved by the look. He could be intimidating and sexy at the same time. She was so nervous she thought she would be sick. He leaned closer to her, his forehead pressed against hers. He stared at her lips for a long time, his warm breath falling on her skin. She knew she couldn't let this happen, but she wasn't moving. She stayed there—waiting.

Coen didn't move, just continued to stare. He pulled away slightly then glanced at her eyes, looking at the vibrant colors then returned his gaze to her lips. He placed his hand on her cheek, his lips only inches away from hers.

Sydney wanted this to happen. Now she was just waiting for it. She hardly knew him, but she wanted to feel the strong connection with him, to release her sexual desire for him. Perhaps it was just lust, but she wanted more of him, all of him. She was so scared to cross the line. There would only be heartbreak and pain on the other side. Knowing this, she still didn't move, waiting to feel his wet lips on hers. She never wanted anything more in her life. The anticipation was more exciting than any intimate touch she had with Aaron. The realization frightened her. Coen made her feel things she'd never experienced. He didn't even have to try. The chemistry was there, surging between them.

Coen looked into her eyes then brought his lips to her cheek, leaving a long kiss on the skin. She felt disappointment as well as relief. He pulled away and looked at her. "I should go if I want to keep my word to you."

"Your word?"

"That I'll be a gentleman."

She felt deflated. Her own emotions were so conflicting that it confused her. She wanted Coen to kiss her as much as she didn't. Perhaps this was best. She seemed to have no sense when it came to him. "Yeah."

He stood up then put his hands in his pocket, walking to the door.

She followed behind him with a heavy heart. She didn't want him to leave, but she knew he should. The sexual tension between them was suffocating the entire room.

"Can I give you a ride to school in the morning then a ride home?"

"Yes," she said quickly, wanting to see him first thing in the morning.

He smiled. "I'll see you then."

"Okay."

He walked out the door then got inside his car.

She watched him from the doorway, staring at the road long after he left. Coen came into her life as quickly as a shooting star. He had always been in her universe, floating by, but now he was so close. She knew her life had changed permanently. Coen would probably break her heart, shattering it worse than Aaron did, but she couldn't stop herself. It was like she didn't have a choice.

# 8

"How'd you sleep?" Coen asked when she got inside the car.

"Good." That was a lie. She dreamt of Coen, waking up with soaked panties and drenched skin. "You?"

"Not so good. I was thinking about you."

That got her interest. "And what were you thinking?"

"That I'm glad you're going on another date with me."

She stared at her hands in her lap. She hoped she wasn't making a huge mistake.

They got to school and parked the car. When they walked to the main building, it was awkward to be side by side with Coen. She had never spent time with him outside the library. The sexual tension was overwhelming no matter where they were. It was in the car, her house, and now under the sun.

His tattoo shined under the light of the sun, the black ink glistening. She thought the marking was hot even though she knew she shouldn't. Guys with tattoos were never good. She had never been attracted to bad boys but she was attracted to Coen. They said nothing as they walked to their classroom. When they got inside, Coen sat in his usual seat across the room. She was a little disappointed.

The day passed and all she thought about was their date that evening. Her friends bugged her about Coen but she kept brushing them off, saying they would discuss it later. She took notes but didn't remember writing them. If the professor called on her to answer a question, she would look like an idiot because she wasn't paying attention.

After class, she tutored Coen, but they didn't open the textbook. He stared at her intently while she spoke, hanging on her every word. It was difficult for her to decipher his expressions. They all looked the same. He always looked sexy and confident, like he had never been embarrassed, humiliated, or ridiculed in his life.

He dropped her off an hour later and said he would return at seven. Instead of studying like she usually did, she rummaged through her closet, looking for something to wear. Normally, she didn't care about her attire. She wore whatever was most comfortable. After trying on a few dresses, she settled on a pair of white shorts with a blue top. Her outfit was ordinary, but she didn't want to make herself seem too eager. She was dressed up anyway.

When she looked in the mirror, she thought about putting on makeup, but she wore so little that she felt weird doing it now. The weight of the cosmetics always made her face feel heavy and painted. She preferred to go natural even though she had been teased about it her whole life. It just wasn't her thing. She styled her hair and gave it a little extra bounce, letting it curl around her shoulders.

She said she would talk to Henry today after school, but she told him she was in a hurry and managed to sneak off with Coen before he found out what was really going on. Since she was excited and happy today, she didn't want to ruin it by breaking Henry's heart.

When the knock sounded on the door, she jumped. It was already seven. Where had the time gone? With a shaky hand, she opened the door.

Coen was wearing jeans and a green shirt. The color highlighted his eyes, making them appear brighter than normal. His arms were bulging with prominence. The lines separating his biceps, triceps, and deltoids were defined. His shirt hung loose around his stomach because his waist and hips were thin. His chest was strong and stood out to her. She knew she was staring, so she averted her gaze. "Hey."

"Hey." He looked at her for a long time, particularly eyeing her legs. "You look nice."

She shrugged. "I just threw this on." She felt stupid for saying that. Why did she always make an idiot of herself around him?

"You're lucky you look good in anything."

She didn't know what to say. Like a smart person, she kept her mouth shut before she said something else stupid.

"Are you ready?"

"Yeah." She grabbed her keys then walked out the door.

He guided her to his car then opened the passenger door for her. She got in and waited for him to walk to the driver's seat. After he got inside, the heated tension was there again, filling the car. She wanted to touch his thigh, his hand—anything. She didn't know what was wrong with her. She wasn't sane when she was around him.

Coen parked the car in front of a restaurant near the beach. It had a large terrace that overlooked the ocean. It looked nice, but not too nice. She was relieved since it was their first—second—date.

"I like this place," he said.

"I'm sure it's great."

He grabbed her hand, sending enough electricity coursing through her body to make her tingle, then led her inside. When they reached the hostess station, he asked for a table on the terrace. He pulled her along as the waitress led them to the patio. There was no one else there. It was just the two of them. The sun was setting over the horizon, making the sky bright with various colors. A slight breeze blew through the strands of her long hair.

Coen pulled out her chair and helped her sit down.

She looked at him in surprise, not expecting him to be so gentle and thoughtful.

When he sat across from her, he looked at her. "Why are you so surprised?"

"What do you mean?"

"I told you I was a gentleman. I meant it."

"Sorry, but you don't always come off that way. Actually, you never come off that way."

"Because I don't treat everyone with the same respect and consideration. Only special people receive such attention."

"Until you get what you want," she blurted.

He glared at her, looking wounded and offended.

Her cheeks reddened. She didn't mean to say that. Now she felt embarrassed. "I'm sorry. It just came out."

He shook his head, saying nothing. He picked up his menu and looked at the selections. She knew she really upset him. The tension was in his shoulders and the anger was evident on his face.

"Coen?"

He didn't look up. "What?"

"I take it back."

"Thank you." He finally met her gaze, looking into her eyes. The intensity of his stare made her look away. She couldn't read him or understand his thoughts, but she couldn't meet his look anyway. It was fierce and powerful. She imagined looking into his eyes when they made love, and the heat spread to her groin then made her spine shiver. She imagined what his naked body looked like then thought about the feel of his tongue on her skin. Inappropriate thoughts sped across her mind, getting dirtier and dirtier. She felt guilty for assuming Coen was just a manwhore when she was clearly the pervert. She couldn't help it. He made her want to do trashy things, forgetting about her reputation and her morals. The area between her legs started to become damp. She crossed her legs and squeezed her thighs together.

"Look at me."

Automatically, she looked up, unable to disobey him.

"What are you thinking about?"

Her cheeks reddened. "Nothing important."

"I'll be the judge of that."

She said nothing for a long time. "What are you going to order?"

"That's what you were thinking about?" he asked incredulously. "Because I was thinking something totally different." His words hung heavily in the air. "I thought we were sharing the same thought."

Now she felt even more embarrassed.

"Would you like to know why I asked you out?"

She really did want to know why. They had the same class together all semester but he never showed any interest in her until she started tutoring him. "I guess."

"You're the most unique person I've ever met."

"How so?"

"You don't wear makeup but you look gorgeous without it. You're natural. I like it."

"So you just like my appearance?"

He smiled. "No, but it is a huge factor. I'm not going to lie. So why did you agree to go out with me?"

She shrugged. "I couldn't say no."

He raised an eyebrow. "I forced you?"

"No. I just couldn't turn you down."

"So you wanted to say no?"

"I should have."

"I don't think so. You won't regret this decision, Syd."

"I hope not," she said quietly.

"I'm really not the asshole that you've depicted."

"My heart is relying on that," she whispered.

He stared into her eyes, the blue color becoming more hypnotic. "No matter what choices you make in life, you're risking a part of yourself. You just have to make sure the jackpot is worth the gamble. If it isn't, then don't risk it."

She crossed her arms over her chest, feeling nervous.

"So, am I worth it, Syd?"

"I—I don't know."

The waitress came and took their orders, interrupting the heated conversation. Sydney hadn't looked at the menu so she opened it and ordered the first vegetarian item she saw. Coen ordered his food then handed over the menus. The waitress walked away and left them alone.

Coen returned his look to her, staring like she was the only thing that existed. She felt like an insect under a magnifying glass, being examined under a high resolution.

The slight curl of her brown hair caught his attention the most. It was soft and silky, never dyed or bleached. He wanted to run his fingers through it, feel every strand. Her skin was a chestnut brown, kissed by the Hawaiian sun. She was perfect in every way, unique in appearance and pure of heart.

"You stare a lot," she whispered.

"People stare at paintings."

"Are you comparing me to a painting?"

"You're my muse."

The compliment caught her off guard. It was the oddest, but sweetest praise she'd ever received. And she least expected it from Coen.

"I could stare at you forever. I would never be bored."

She felt the same way but would never admit it. Not yet, at least.

The waitress brought their dishes and placed them on the table. Coen placed his napkin on his lap then started to eat. His movements were so precise that he looked elegant, refined. He had perfect manners and ate like it was a profession. He didn't inhale his food like most men, but chewed every bite and enjoyed it.

Sydney ate less than she normally did. She was too nervous around Coen. When she watched him eat, she wondered how her tongue would feel next to his. His wet kiss on her skin would feel so hot it would burn her entirely. When her thoughts turned naughtier, him lying on top of her with her legs spread, she shook her head. She couldn't think about that right now. She was disgusting.

"What?"

"Huh?"

"Why'd you shake your head?"

"I...I don't know."

He raised an eyebrow. "Okay..."

She poked her food again.

"You're so different around me."

"I'm just quiet."

"No, you aren't. A shy girl doesn't take self-defense classes and fight better than most men. You could kick my dad's ass if you wanted."

She said nothing, knowing she was stuck in a lie.

"I think you were thinking about something else."

She looked out at the ocean, staring at the setting sun. She wanted to stare at Coen, seeing his beautiful face and his prominent cheekbones.

"Fine. I'll discover all your secrets eventually."

"Why did you choose marine biology?" she asked, trying to change the subject. She would never admit the truth—that she thought about fucking him all day, every day.

"I like animals. I think they're awesome. I've been obsessed since I was little. In third grade, we learned about all mammals, insects, arachnids, reptiles, and dinosaurs and I was totally hooked. I'm not ashamed to admit I still have all my dinosaur figurines."

That made her smile. "I was obsessed with dinosaurs too. I was teased for being a tomboy."

He rolled his eyes. "Kids are stupid. They'll rip you apart for being different in the slightest way. After pulling your hair and stealing your lunch, I would have shared my toys with you," he said with wink.

"My dad and I saw Jurassic Park together when it came out. I made him take me five times."

He laughed. "I did the same thing. And when it came out on video, I watched it like a million times. Don't worry. You aren't the only loser."

"I didn't say I was a loser."

"Well, you were. We both were."

"I guess it's a little better if I'm not the only one. So what do you want to do with your degree?"

He shrugged. "I don't know. I'm not going to pretend that I know what I'm doing. I think most people are clueless."

"Well, it's either research or teaching, right?"

"Or dolphin training."

She stared at him, her heart falling.

He caught her serious expression. "Syd, that was a joke. I would never do that. I may eat animals but I respect them."

She breathed a sigh of relief. She taught Rose a few tricks, but she would never become a trainer. Aquariums and zoos were disgusting to her. She hated keeping the beautiful creatures locked up and away from their natural habitat, but she knew it was inevitable. That's the only reason she was able to work at the aquarium. She did her best to make it clean and pleasant for the wildlife there. Her respect for animals was the foundation of her spirituality. She could never be with someone who didn't uphold the same values.

"I didn't mean to offend you. Since you work at the aquarium, I assumed you'd enjoy the joke."

"You didn't," she said quickly.

She was done so she placed her napkin on the table. Then she stared at him, sneaking in a long look of his features. He was watching the ocean, finally focused on something other than her. She took advantage of the opportunity to capture his handsome features, his chiseled jaw and his kissable lips. She loved everything about his physicality but she loved his eyes the most. Every time she looked at them, she thought of the ocean, the most mysterious thing on the planet.

The waitress brought the check and placed it on the table. Coen slipped the money inside before Sydney could even move. She wanted to offer to leave the tip but decided not to. She could tell Coen would never allow that.

"Thank you for dinner," she said.

"You're very welcome." He stood up then pulled her chair out, helping her stand up. He grabbed her hand, and she immediately felt the rush inside her body. She loved touching him, having a hold on him. As he walked her back to the car, she was in a daze, feeling a variety of emotions.

He opened the door for her like he always did, allowing her to get inside first.

As Coen drove down the road, Sydney kept glancing at him, seeing his profile from the light of the dashboard. Her attraction to him was driving her crazy. She loved everything about him, his personality as well as his looks. But the fear was always in the back of her mind— that it wouldn't last.

When they arrived at the house, she felt her heart hammer in her chest. She didn't want their date to end. He walked her to the front door, his hands in his pockets. He stopped when they reached her door. It didn't seem like he had any intention of coming inside.

He looked at her. "I think you're breathtaking, sexy, and beautiful. When I look at your legs, I want to run my hands across them, from the bottom of your toes up to your ass. I want to kiss your inner thighs and taste you. When I look at your hips, I think about kissing the skin above the brim of your shorts. Your hair reminds me of the sun on a bright day, shiny and bright. My fingers want to run through the strands until they stop on your neck, feeling the slender curves of your body. And when I look at your lips, I think of a million things. I want to feel every curve of the skin, taste the flavor of your ChapStick and suck them until they are dry. When I look into your eyes, I never want to look away. That's what I was thinking about, Syd. Just in case you were wondering."

She was speechless, not expecting such a detailed recollection of his thoughts. It made her feel flattered and embarrassed at the same time.

He continued to stare at her. "Now, what were you thinking about?"

She searched for the right words for a long time. "You wanna come inside?"

He smiled. "I thought so." He came forward, pushing her against the door.

She turned around, shoving her key in the door and opening it. She walked inside and felt him behind her. She moved into the living room then sat down on the couch, feeling her heart in her chest, fluttering wildly. No one ever made her so nervous. Normally, she was calm and collected, not a blundering idiot.

He sat beside her, seeming relaxed. "What do you want to do?"

The question surprised her. She thought he knew what she wanted to do. "I guess we can watch a movie."

"Do you want to watch a movie?"

She had no interest in watching a movie. She wanted him to kiss her, but at the same time, she didn't want him to. Her insecurities and fear were competing with her desire at equal force. But when she looked at his lips, she had one thing on her mind. "No."

"Good. Because I really want to kiss you."

She closed her eyes and took a deep breath, winded by his words. He leaned forward and rubbed his nose against hers, staring into her eyes. One hand glided up her arm then entered her hair, pulling a few strands back. He stared at her lips for a long time but did nothing.

"I can't," she whispered.

"Why?"

"I don't trust myself with you."

He smiled. "I like what I'm hearing."

"I'm being serious."

He pulled away slightly. "I won't kiss you if you don't want me to, but please tell me why you don't want me to."

She averted her gaze. "I'm really...really attracted to you. And I just...don't want this to go somewhere too quickly. I know that as soon as I kiss you, I'm going to be completely reckless and stupid, doing things I'm not ready for."

He said nothing for a moment, his blue eyes locked onto her green ones. "How far would you like to go? What is your limit?"

"Why?"

"I promise that we won't pass it, no matter how hot and heavy we become. You can lose yourself in me and I won't betray your request. You can be free, enjoying the moment without the fear of losing control. Put your trust in me."

She bit her lip. "I want to kiss you."

"Is that all?"

"I want to see you with your clothes off."

"Okay. Can I take off yours?"

She nodded.

"What else can I do?"

"I want you to get me off."

"So I can finger you?"

"Yeah."

"Can you get me off?"

She nodded.

"Can I go down on you?"

"No," she said quietly.

"Can we have anal sex?" he asked with a wink.

"You wish."

"Vaginal?"

She shook her head.

"Okay. I can remember all that."

"I'm normally not like this," she whispered. "I don't do stuff like this."

"Like what?"

"Fool around with someone I'm not in a relationship with."

"Do you want to be in a relationship with me?"

"Isn't that too soon?"

"I really like you, Sydney. I really doubt I'm going to start liking you less. If anything, I'm going to fall for you. I don't mind being in a committed relationship. You can trust me to be faithful to you and I trust you to do the same, even if it is a secret."

"I'm scared."

"Why?"

She said nothing.

"Because Aaron cheated on you? That guy is an idiot. I would never do that."

"Promise me?"

He rubbed his nose against hers then placed her hand over his heart. "I swear to you, Sydney, that I will not cheat on you, lie to you, unless it's in your best interest or I'm trying to surprise you, and I will do my best to not hurt you. I can't promise that I won't because that's impossible, but I will do my best not to."

She pressed her forehead against his. "Okay."

He smiled. "But this can't be a secret for long, okay? I want everyone to know that I'm taken."

"Okay. I'll try."

He cupped her cheek then pressed his face close to hers. She felt her heart hammer in her chest like it would explode. She had fantasized about kissing those lips so many times. Now they were just an inch away. When they kissed she knew she would fall for him, wanting him all the time.

He leaned in and pressed his lips against hers gently. His breath filled her lungs as he caressed her lips with his mouth. She responded to him, tasting the sweetness of his tongue. When he slipped his tongue inside her, she moaned, running her fingers through the strands of his hair. It was soft and silky. She ran her fingers down his chest and over his stomach, feeling his muscled frame. She already felt aroused to the point of breaking. There was a fire she never felt before, a longing that never circulating through her, igniting everything in its path. She never felt that way with Aaron even though she enjoyed their time together. This was a completely different experience.

Coen lay her down on the couch then crawled on top of her. She opened her legs to him, wrapping them around his waist. Her hands were running over his body wildly, feeling him everywhere. His shirt was torn away and she stared at his body for a moment. He kissed her forehead while she gazed.

She kissed him again while she unbuttoned his jeans, excited to see the bottom half. When she felt his erection, she knew he was big. She wanted to see just how big he could be. She pulled his jeans down his hips to his ankles. He kicked them off once they hit the ground.

She grabbed his briefs and pulled them down too. He broke their kiss and watched her expression while she revealed him. It was like Christmas morning.

"Oh god," she whispered.

"You like what you see?"

She moaned then pulled his briefs down all the way. "You're so—god."

"I'm excited to see you."

"I can tell."

"I really hope so," he said with a light laugh.

She continued to run her hands up and down his body. "You're the sexiest thing I've ever seen."

He pressed his mouth over hers then unbuttoned her shorts. He pulled them off but left her underwear on. He grabbed her shirt then removed it, leaving her bra. He unclasped that then dropped it to the floor. "Holy shit," he said.

"You like what you see?" she asked.

"I wanna fuck you—hard."

She grabbed his face and kissed him. "You should. Please. I want you."

He pulled off her underwear then pressed his body against hers. His erection was the length of her stomach. She hadn't been with anyone as big as him. She hoped it wouldn't be a problem. And after not having sex for six months, she knew she would be tight again.

He leaned over and sucked her nipples while she reached down and stroked him. He moaned as he felt her move up and down his shaft. "Fuck."

She grabbed his neck and kissed him there, trailing kisses to his ear. "Please, please."

"What about your limits?"

"Fuck what I said."

"This is more difficult than I thought it was going to be."

She wrapped her legs around his waist, pulling him closer to her entrance.

"You're gonna make me come just by doing this," he whispered.

"I had a dream about you. You were fucking me everywhere in the house, pounding into me as hard as you could, and I came harder than I ever have in my life. I want to do that now. Fuck me, Coen."

He closed his eyes and pressed his forehead against hers. After a moment, he reached his hand down and started to rub her clit. "Do you finger yourself?"

"No."

"This is going to be quick then."

She grabbed his shoulders and dug her nails into the skin, feeling the pleasure throb inside of her.

He slipped two fingers within her, feeling the inside of her soaked pussy. While he moved inside her, he rubbed her clit more aggressively.

"I can already feel it," she whispered.

He pressed his forehead against hers while he moved into her harder.

"Oh—god!"

His thumb moved faster.

"Yeah—oh—don't stop." She held him tighter. "Please don't stop." She leaned her head back as the momentum came into her body then left a moment later. Her frame was shaken by the force of the impact. She felt her body revive after the long absence of touch. "Coen."

He pulled his fingers out. "I know I said I would be a gentleman, but please get me off."

"It would be my pleasure."

"Do you have Vaseline or lotion?"

"Both."

"Can you get the Vaseline?"

"Yeah."

He rose from her body and let her get up. She stumbled down the hallway, not accustomed to her post orgasm fatigue, then grabbed the jar under the sink. When she came back into the room, he stared at her with a hungry expression. Seeing his hard-on made her aroused again. She opened the lid and grabbed a scoop. She straddled his hips and rubbed the Vaseline up and down his shaft.

He bit his lip while he felt her. He grabbed her tits and squeezed them while she jerked him as hard as she could. His hands slid down to her ass and he fingered again from behind. She moaned as she felt him inside her. The harder he fingered her, the harder she stroked him.

"I need you to come again," he said between heavy breaths.

"Yeah—okay." She squeezed his cock harder as she jerked him.

He moved his fingers inside of her faster.

She pressed her forehead against his. "Now. I'm coming now."

He let go as she cried his name. He shot on her breasts and stomach, and it felt so good on the way out. It almost made him cry it was so amazing. He leaned back against the couch and closed his eyes. "Holy shit."

She closed her eyes and said nothing.

"Amazing."

She moaned.

He rose from the couch then walked into the bathroom. After we wiped himself off, he returned with a towel and cleaned her up. "Sorry about the mess," he said.

"That was so hot."

He smiled. "I know it was." He sat beside her and placed her in his lap. "We can't do it again though."

"What? Why?"

"I thought I could control myself but I can't. That's never happened before."

"What do you mean?"

"When you asked me to fuck you, I almost did. I promised you that I wouldn't. I don't think I can keep that promise if I'm in the same situation."

She leaned against him. "I don't know if I want you to keep that promise."

"We aren't having sex yet. Not until this Henry thing gets cleared up and we've known each other for a while."

"Why?"

"Because I really care about you and I don't want to lose you. I want to wait."

"So we can't do anything?"

"We can kiss but we can't get naked anymore, otherwise I'll have a slip up."

She sighed. "Damn."

"I need to get dressed before my boner returns."

She whined. "I love seeing you naked."

"I'll send you some naked pics and you can masturbate to them."

"I don't masturbate."

"Why?"

"I just can't come that way."

"Really?"

She nodded.

"I'll show you."

"You will?"

"I don't want you to be sexually frustrated the entire time we're together."

"Or you could just do it."

"I can try but if you ask me to fuck you, I will. I think it's best if we don't go down that road."

"Okay."

After he was dressed, he sat back down. "You need to get dressed too."

She sighed. "Fine." She pulled on her clothes then sat on the couch.

"Well, we can watch a movie or go out and get your car."

"What do you mean?"

"Since we have a secret relationship, I can't drive you to school so we need to get it now."

"But it doesn't work."

He smiled. "I took off the distributor cap."

Her eyes widened. "What?"

"Sorry. I wanted to spend more time with you if our date went well. I was going to tell you the truth."

"What happened to your promise?"

"Well, I did it before the promise, and even if I didn't, I had your best interest at heart so I'm vindicated either way."

She shook her head. "I can't believe you did that."

"And look where it got us?"

"You're lucky I'm not pissed."

"That's probably because I gave you an orgasm."

"Well, you would have been in deep shit if you didn't."

"That wasn't going to happen. I'll always please you."

She smiled. "That sounds nice."

"So you want to get your car?"

"Yes. Let's go."

They returned to his car and he held the door open for her, helping her climb inside. After he was in the driver's seat, he patted the middle seat. "This is the girlfriend seat. You belong over here."

She smiled then scooted next to him. "I like this seat."

He kissed her on the forehead. "Good." He started the engine then placed his arm over the backseat. They drove straight to her car. It was dark outside so Coen had to use a flashlight to return the part to the engine.

"You better fix it," she said as she watched him.

He twisted the cap then closed the hood, wiping his hands on his pants. "It's as good as new."

"It better be."

He smiled. "I guess I'll see you tomorrow at school."

"I thought you were going to come back over."

"Do you want me to?"

"Duh."

He smiled. "Then I will."

He walked her to the driver's side then helped her get in. They left the parking lot and returned to the shack on the beach. When they came back into the house, they cuddled under a blanket together and watched television.

Sydney hadn't felt this whole and complete since Aaron was her boyfriend. She wasn't sure if she could trust Coen but she decided to take a chance anyway. She was drawn to him like she was to no one else. Even if he was a cheating asshole, she would still be sitting on that couch, her legs intertwined around his, her hand placed over his beating heart.

# 9

Her friends cornered her the next morning, pulling everything out of her.

"How long was he there for?" Henry asked.

Sydney was distracted, thinking about kissing Coen, so she didn't hear his question.

"Sydney?"

"Sorry. What?"

"Coen. How long was he there for?"

"Coen came to your house? Why?" Nancy asked, her eyes wide.

"Well, my car wouldn't start so he gave me a ride home."

"But didn't you have dinner too?" Henry asked.

Nancy raised an eyebrow. "You made him dinner?"

"I didn't want to be rude," she said quickly.

"So you guys are friends now?" Nancy asked.

"Yeah. I think so." They definitely didn't act like friends, but she wasn't going to tell them that. She had never fooled around like that before. It was like her lips were inflamed with poison, burning even after the kiss was long over. And his naked body—she couldn't think about that right now. She didn't bring any extra underwear. She wondered if they had moved too fast, but she didn't have any regrets. She was so hot for him that she didn't care.

They walked inside the science building and entered their classroom. Coen was already sitting in his seat, his shirt loose from his stomach. He was looking at his phone, his arms large and flexed. His tattoo shined under the florescent lights.

Sydney sat down and stared at him, her lips slightly open. She couldn't believe Coen was her boyfriend—her secret boyfriend. They just started talking and now they were—together. It seemed odd. She was supposed to just tutor him but her brain had other plans. She waited for him to look at her but he never did. He completely ignored her. That's what she wanted him to do but she couldn't help but feel disappointed.

Henry leaned close to her. "Can I borrow a pencil?"

She reached into her backpack and handed it to him. "Just keep it, Henry."

"Really?"

"You ask to borrow it every period so just hold onto it."

He dropped it on top of his notebook and leaned back. "So, you wanna get some dinner and sit on the beach tonight?" he asked.

Coen looked over when he heard him. Sydney felt his stare but she didn't meet his gaze. She knew she had to talk to Henry and make it clear she didn't see him in a romantic way—that she didn't love him. "Actually, I wanted to talk to you about something."

"Oh? What?"

"Meet me at my place tonight."

He smiled. "I'll be there."

Nancy raised an eyebrow when she looked at Sydney but she didn't say anything. Coen finally looked away.

Professor Jones came into the classroom and handed back their exams. Henry and Nancy both got Cs. They were totally ecstatic.

"Yes! I passed," Henry boomed.

"I didn't fail!" Nancy squealed.

Sydney turned her paper facedown so no one could see it. She looked over at Coen and saw his blank test. It had a zero written in red next to his name. He had been too distracted to take the exam and now she wondered what had been on his mind.

Professor Jones took back the exams then started the lecture on new material. Sydney took out her notebook and started to scribble away, relieved to be distracted from Coen, her hot boyfriend that she wanted to see naked again. Her cheeks blushed every time she thought about it. He was definitely good with his hands.

When the period ended, Coen dashed out the door without looking back. Sydney was sad that she wouldn't see him until their tutoring session that afternoon. She wondered if they would even study or just make out the whole time. She hoped it was the latter.

She and Henry went to their next class and sat in the back row. She dreaded seeing Henry later that evening. She knew she was going to rip his heart out. Why hadn't she noticed his feelings before? Why was she so blind? It's totally obvious.

When they met for lunch in the cafeteria, Henry grabbed his food then returned to the table, handing Sydney a salad and some assorted fruit.

"What's this for?" she asked.

"It's lunchtime. I assumed you were hungry," Henry said with a smile. He picked up his pizza and took a bite.

"You don't need to buy me food, Henry."

"I know. I just thought it would be convenient since I was over there." He looked up at her. "I hope that's okay."

"Just don't do it again," she snapped.

He flinched. "I'm...sorry."

Nancy looked at them then averted her gaze, uncomfortable by the direction of the conversation.

She sighed. "I'm sorry, Henry. I didn't mean to snap at you. Just ignore me."

"Is everything okay?" he asked.

"Yes, it's fine. I'm sorry."

"It's okay," he said quietly. "I'll be right back. I need to get some napkins." He left the table and walked to the other side of the room.

"What was that?" Nancy asked.

"I just don't want him to buy my food."

"Why?"

"I don't want him to get the wrong idea."

She leaned forward, her eyes bright. "You know?"

She nodded.

"When did you figure it out?"

"Have you known this whole time?" she asked angrily.

"Are you kidding me? Everyone knows!"

"Well, I didn't."

"Because you're blind."

"How long?"

"Since the day he met you, Syd."

Sydney covered her face with her hands. "Damn."

"What are you going to do?"

"I'll talk to him today."

"And say what?"

"That it's not going to happen."

"It's not?" she asked sadly.

"No."

Nancy looked at her uneaten pizza for a moment then returned her gaze to Sydney. "Why not?"

"I...I just don't feel that way about him."

"Why? He's really cute."

"Of course he is. But I just see him as a friend."

"Well, if you gave him a chance, you might feel differently."

She immediately thought of her feelings for Coen. She would never feel the same way about Henry. "No."

Nancy sighed. "It's going to break his heart."

"I know."

"What are you going to say?"

"The truth."

"Be easy, okay?"

"Of course. I love him."

"I would hate to be him today."

Coen dropped into the seat across from Nancy, startling both women. "Hey there." He placed a book on the table along with a sandwich.

Sydney wasn't sure what to do. "Uh, hi."

"Cool if I sit with you guys?" he asked as he unwrapped his sandwich.

"Sure," Sydney said hesitantly.

Coen bit into his sandwich and chewed while he turned the pages of his textbook. His blue eyes were startling, like always. The muscles in his forearms flexed as he held his sandwich. His shirt clung tightly to his shoulders.

"Why are you sitting with us?" Nancy asked.

Coen answered her without meeting her gaze. "Sydney and I are friends." He looked at Sydney. "Right?"

"Yeah. We're friends," she said awkwardly.

He looked back at Nancy. "How did you do on Jones's exam?" He acted like she wasn't incredibly rude just a second ago.

She shrugged. "I got a C."

"At least you passed."

"Did you just zone out?"

"I just couldn't concentrate at the time. Sydney has been helping with that."

She nodded. "Okay."

Nancy wasn't used to his vague sentences but Sydney was. She wanted to know why he was spending time with her and her friends but she couldn't ask him right then. It would have to wait.

Henry returned to the table and stared at Coen for a moment before he sat across from Sydney.

Coen nodded to him. "Hey, man."

Henry nodded but didn't say anything. Sydney knew he didn't like Coen but she wasn't sure why. Coen had always been nice to both of her friends.

"How did you do on the test?" Coen asked, looking at Henry.

He ate his pizza without looking at him. "I passed."

"Cool," he said. "I didn't."

"I assumed."

The table fell silent.

Coen looked at Sydney and held her gaze for a moment. She wished her two friends weren't there, or better yet, they knew what Coen meant to her. She didn't like keeping him a secret and she knew he was equally frustrated. He was just an outsider to them.

"So, why are you here?" Henry asked.

"Sydney is my friend. I thought we could hang out."

"She has plenty of friends," he said quietly.

Sydney's eyes widened. Now that she knew Henry was in love with her, she noticed his obvious jealousy and possessiveness of her. How was she so stupid before? "I invited him," she said quickly.

Coen smiled at her, pleased by her defense of him. She knew how annoyed he was by the secrecy so she had to defend him in some way.

Henry raised an eyebrow. "I apologize. I didn't know."

"It's okay," she said quietly.

Coen read his textbook while he ate his lunch slowly. He was very particular in his movement, not spilling any crumbs or making a mess in any way. His mouth was clean when he was finished. He didn't even need a napkin. Sydney wished she could kiss those lips, taste the mustard from his mouth. He glanced up at her and smiled, noticing her look, then returned his attention to the table.

Henry noticed her stare but didn't comment.

"So, are you going to Liz's party this weekend?" Nancy asked.

"That depends," Coen said. "Are you guys going?" His gaze was directed at Sydney.

"Yeah," Nancy said. "She really wants us to be there."

Sydney nodded. "We'll probably just make an appearance."

"Well, I might stop by then," he said.

Nancy nodded. "Cool."

Sydney glanced at Nancy, noticing her direct stare. She better not be checking out her boyfriend. That would just make her mad. But Sydney knew she had no right to be upset at her friend. It wasn't Nancy's fault that she was ignorant to Coen's commitment to Sydney.

"So where's your girlfriend?" Nancy asked.

"Audrey isn't my girlfriend," he said calmly. His jaw was tense, and Sydney knew he was trying to hold his anger back. He hated talking about her. She also noticed how he never said he didn't have a girlfriend, just that she wasn't Audrey.

"Well, I saw you with her this weekend," Nancy said.

"No. You saw me running from her," Coen said. "You misinterpreted the situation entirely."

"So you just broke up?"

"No. We've been broken up for four months."

"Four months?" she asked incredulously. "That can't be right."

"We officially broke up two months ago, but the relationship was dead before that final break. She has separation issues."

"So what happened? You cheat on her?"

He glared at Nancy. Sydney knew he wanted to snap. She wondered if he would hold his tongue. Coen took a deep breath. "No. That isn't my style. She and I just couldn't work it out."

"But I know you slept with Tawny a few months ago."

"When I was single, free to do whatever I wanted," he said.

"So you sleep around?"

"This conversation has gone on long enough. No further questions, please."

Sydney was shocked that he put up with it at all. It was obvious how uncomfortable he was.

Nancy leaned forward. "So, are you looking for someone new?"

Sydney didn't like the direction of the conversation.

"No," Coen said. "I'm not looking for a girlfriend."

"So you just want to have fun?"

"No. I'm happy with my life the way it is."

"So—"

"Nancy," Sydney said. "Please stop interrogating my friend."

"I'm not interrogating him," she snapped.

"Yeah, you are," Henry said. "Back off."

Nancy sat back in her chair and crossed her arms over her chest.

Sydney knew she came off a little strong sometimes, asking information that was none of her business. She didn't mean to be rude and had good intentions. But it didn't always come out that way.

Sydney looked at Coen. "I apologize. She meant well."

He smiled and she felt her heart pound in her chest. "It's fine."

Nancy looked away.

Coen leaned toward her. "So, how's your day been?"

She smiled, her stomach rising to her mouth and her legs becoming weak. "It was good. How was yours?"

"It was alright."

She picked up her fork and picked at her mixed fruit.

He grabbed a grape and tossed it into his mouth. "Yum."

She stared at his lips, wanting to taste the sugar on his tongue. When she felt her cheeks turn red, she changed her thoughts and looked away.

Coen stared at her, obviously noticing the change of color in her face. He didn't comment on it. "Well, I need to get to class." He put his book in his bag and stood up. "I'll see you later," he said to Sydney.

She didn't want him to go. "Okay."

He nodded to her friends. "I'll see you guys later."

Henry nodded and Nancy waved.

Sydney watched him walk out of the cafeteria. His absence left a hole in her heart. She hated hiding him from her friends. She wanted everyone to know that he was hers. But when she thought of Henry, she knew she couldn't do that. That would be too much information at one time. His brain might explode.

"You guys getting close?" Henry asked.

Sydney adjusted herself in her seat. "We've become good friends."

"What's his tattoo mean?" Nancy asked.

"I don't know. I've never asked."

"Tattoos are lame," Henry said.

"I like them," Sydney blurted.

"Oh. I guess they are cool," he said.

She realized if she told him murdering people was cool, he would probably agree with her. He would agree with anything she said. Their talk that afternoon was going to really suck. "I need to get to lab," she said as she shouldered her backpack.

Henry grabbed his stuff. "Me too."

"See ya," she said to Nancy.

"Bye," Nancy said to them both.

110

She and Henry walked back to the science building together. The humidity drenched her skin and made her hair shine. She never grew tired of the tropical climate. Even winters in California were too cold for her.

His shoulder touched hers when they walked. She stepped away so they wouldn't be so close. Since they had every class together, she knew the rest of the week would be awkward after she told him how she felt. She wished she wasn't so ignorant and didn't let it get this bad. She could have stopped it a long time ago.

They both went to lab and spent the next three hours finishing their experiments. She didn't mind having him as a partner because he always gave his best effort, but he usually messed something up or used the equipment incorrectly. Science wasn't his forte. She wasn't sure why he majored in it. He wasn't stupid, far from it, but he was better suited to English, Psychology, and Sociology. His mind worked differently than hers. But if zoology was what he wanted to do, she wouldn't tell him not to.

When the class was over, they left the building and walked outside.

"So, what time do you want me to come over?" he asked with a smile.

She knew he thought this was going to be a good night. That assumption couldn't be more wrong. "Seven?"

"I'll be there. Do you need company on your way to the library?"

"No, I'm good. I'll see you later, Henry."

"Okay." He turned around and walked to the parking lot in front of the building.

She sighed then headed toward the library. Her excitement at seeing Coen was ruined by the stress and guilt she felt in the pit of her stomach. What was she going to say to Henry? It seemed like she was going to lose her friend either way.

Her feet carried her through the library until she reached the study room they always worked in. The window to the room was covered with a curtain. She opened the door and looked for Coen. He was sitting in his usual spot.

He stood up. "Hey."

She shut the door behind her. "Hi."

He wrapped his arms around her waist and kissed her gently on the mouth, making her melt immediately. "I've wanted to do that all day."

She smiled at him, frozen to the spot. He made her feel tingly and wild.

He grabbed her hand and dragged her to the chair, pulling her in his lap. He rubbed his nose against hers. "You ready to study?"

"It doesn't seem like we are going to be doing much of it."

"Oh, we will."

"Really?" she said with a smile. She couldn't stop grinning. She was starting to feel like a hanger was lodged in her mouth.

"Today we'll be studying the anatomy of the mouth." He cupped her cheek then placed this thumb on her bottom lip. "Particularly the lip and the tongue."

"I must have missed that lecture."

"Well, I'll catch you up." He leaned in and kissed her gently.

A moan immediately escaped her lips, out of her control. She felt his tongue slip inside her mouth and caress her gently. When his hand ran up her back then through her hair, she felt her logical thought slip away. Her hands rubbed his chest, feeling the muscles underneath. His hot breaths filled her mouth and burned her lungs.

All she felt in that moment was Coen. All other thoughts ceased. Only his lips and body mattered. She wasn't thinking about Henry, school, work, or her friends.

It was just Coen. When she kissed Aaron, she enjoyed it, but it wasn't anything like this. She felt connected to him, physically and spiritually. With every passing kiss, she felt herself fall for him. The depth was so deep that she would never be able to crawl out. He crippled her entire body, making her hungry for him alone.

The time passed in a flash. Neither one of them broke their kiss to speak or do anything else. Their textbooks remained zipped in their backpacks, forgotten. Sydney ran her fingers through his hair, feeling the slight curl at the end, and breathed into his mouth, losing her control. He pulled her closer to him and continued to devour her mouth, unable to satisfy his need for her. When his watch beeped, she knew the session was over.

Reluctantly, he pulled away. "Time for work," he whispered through his heavy breathing.

She placed her forehead against his. "Damn."

He kissed her gently on the lips once more. "My lips are dry."

"If we keep this up, we're going to need some serious ChapStick."

"Or Vaseline."

She smiled. "I know you like Vaseline."

"I went through a jar last night from thinking of you."

She felt the area between her legs burn. "That's so hot."

"I'm glad you don't think it's gross."

She licked her lips. "Definitely not."

"Do you think about me?"

"Yes, but I haven't done anything."

"That's right. I'll have to show you."

"Good."

He pressed his forehead against hers then ran his fingers through his hair. "We should go."

"Yeah."

"Could you get off me and give me a second?"

"Massive hard-on?"

"I'm about to explode," he said with a laugh.

She got up and grabbed her bag from the ground. He looked at his phone for a moment before he rose from his chair and walked out the door. As they walked through the lobby, he grabbed her hand.

She pulled away. "We can't do that."

"Why? We aren't going to see anyone we know."

"That doesn't mean someone we know won't see us."

"Fine," he snapped.

"Please don't be angry."

"I won't put up with this for long," he warned. "If I'm your boyfriend, I want everyone to know it."

"Soon, okay?"

"Better be."

They left the library then approached the parking lot.

"Let's carpool," he said.

"Okay."

He opened the passenger door and helped her get inside. When she buckled her safety belt, he kissed her then shut the door. She watched him walk around the car, looking at his straight back and swinging arms. When he got inside, he released her safety belt and pulled her to the middle seat.

"This is the girlfriend seat," he said.

She smiled. "I forgot."

"Don't forget again. That's where you belong." He wrapped his arm around her shoulder then backed out of the parking lot. She leaned into him and placed her hand on his thigh.

"I'm sorry Nancy was so rude," she said.

He smiled. "It's fine. I get that a lot."

"People ask you about Audrey?"

"Girls usually do. I don't mean to sound like a dick, but I think Nancy has a thing for me."

"I thought the same thing."

He sighed. "I really wish I could tell her who my girlfriend is."

"I know."

"Are you pissed at her?"

"It's not her fault."

"You didn't even tell her you were attracted to me?"

"I did."

"So aren't I yours, then?"

"Well, I also said I wouldn't date you because you weren't boyfriend material."

"She's going to be in for a surprise."

"Yeah."

"Good luck with that," he said. "And I am boyfriend material."

"I hope so."

He kissed her on the forehead. "I'll prove it."

"Okay."

They arrived at the gym then got out.

"Isn't this against the rules or something?" she asked.

"What?"

"Being involved with your client?"

"No. And it wouldn't matter anyway."

She smiled. "Good to know." She grabbed her bag then walked inside with him. "I'll be there in a second," she said as she entered the changing room. After she pulled her hair into a ponytail and slipped on her workout clothes, she stared at herself in the mirror. She had a flat stomach that was tone and firm, but she felt like her body wasn't as strong or powerful as the rest of the women at the gym. She was still an amateur. She left the locker room then entered the studio.

Just like last time, Coen had his shirt off.

She stared at him, her mouth gaping open.

"Can never get enough, huh?" he said with a laugh.

She composed herself. "It's just distracting."

"Not as distracting as you."

"What?"

"You know how hard it is to train someone while having a boner the whole time?"

"You see girls in tights and a sports bra all the time. You should be used to it."

He laughed. "I'm definitely not used to your hot bod. You are ridiculously sexy."

She looked down at herself. "You don't think I'm too—muscular?"

He stepped toward her and looked down at her body. "Definitely not. I like that you're muscular. I hate chicks that are too skinny and they purposely only drink water and eat saltines to stay that way." He grabbed her thigh. "You're strong, Sydney. That's hot." He lightly hit her stomach with the back of his palm. "I love it." He leaned over and looked around her. "Don't even get me started on your ass."

She blushed. "I always thought I was too big."

"Hell no. You're perfect, baby. A dime."

"What's a dime?"

"You've never been called that before?"

"No."

"It's slang for saying you're a perfect ten."

"Oh."

"Actually, you're a quarter."

"Well, thanks."

"Anytime," he said as he grabbed the remote and looked at her. When he crossed his arms over his chest, she knew he was being serious. "So, are you going to tell me?"

"Huh?"

"Who are you afraid of?"

She looked away. "No one."

He stepped in front of her, leaning down to be in her line of sight. "How can I help you if I don't know what you need?"

"Just train me to fight."

"You already know how. Help me help you. Now tell me."

"I already said no."

He sighed. "You're pissing me off."

"The feeling is mutual."

"Will you ever tell me?"

"No."

"Is it Aaron?"

"Of course not."

"An ex-boyfriend?"

"No."

"Tell me!"

"No!" She tightened her gloves on her hands. "It just makes me feel better knowing I can defend myself if I ever need to. I can sleep at night knowing I'm not completely defenseless. That's all you need to know."

"So no one is threatening you in the present time?"

She was quiet for a moment. "No."

He breathed a sigh of relief. "Okay."

She said nothing.

"If you're ever scared, you can always call me. You know that, right?"

She nodded. "Yes."

"Even if it's just to talk."

"I know that too."

"Okay." He pressed the button on the remote. "Let's begin."

# 10

"I'm going to train you with weapons," he said.

"Weapons?" she asked, frightened. "Why?"

"Well, whoever it is you're afraid of might attack you with a weapon. What would you do then?"

"Run."

"And what if you can't?"

She felt her heart accelerate. "I—I don't know."

"I thought not." He walked away and grabbed a bat from the corner. He spun it in his wrist while he looked at her.

She immediately stepped back, her vision blurring. The snap of the wood as it collided against her ribs rang in her ears. The way it thudded against the ground as it landed on the tile flooded her mind. The blood stains were etched into her memory. Sweat dripped from her forehead and formed on her palms. She stared at the bat and felt her stomach jump in her throat.

He stared at her, watching her every move. His jaw was clenched tight and there was anger in his eyes. "You've been attacked with a bat before."

She said nothing.

He looked away and closed his eyes, breathing through the pain in his heart. His arms shook with uncontrollable ferocity. "Who did that to you?"

She ignored him as she stared at the bat. She didn't want him to know how scared she was, but she couldn't hide her fear. The weapon represented more than just pain.

"Sydney, you should tell the police."

"Just stop it, okay?" she snapped.

He sighed. "Let's begin."

She stepped back with her hands raised. "No. Stop."

He froze. "Why?"

"I just—no."

118

He gripped the bat. "What if it happens again, Sydney? What will you do?"

"I don't know."

He marched to her then stopped before her. She avoided his gaze, staring at his chest. "This will happen. I refuse not to help you."

"I don't want to use a bat."

"Too bad. You will overcome this."

"I can't."

"Be strong, Sydney. I will sleep better knowing that you can defeat me. Do this for me."

"I'm scared."

"I won't hurt you. I promise."

She started breathing heavily, feeling her chest rise and fall with every breath. "You won't?"

"Never."

"Okay."

He kissed her on the forehead. "Thank you."

She nodded.

Coen stepped back. "Let's start."

Coen chased her while he swung the bat, teaching her to miss his strikes and avoid his blows. He never hit her, always deflecting his blows before they touched her skin. He knew she was frightened by the look in her eyes, but she trusted him more. Whatever happened to her was enough to make her appear weak, something he had never seen before.

The hour went by and he trained her to confiscate the weapon from his hands, hurting him in the process. After she felt more proficient in the task, she started to calm down. At first, she wouldn't even touch the bat, avoiding it at all costs. When she finally got her hands on it, she held it in her grasp for a long time, saying nothing.

When they were finished, he put the bat into the cupboard. As soon as it was out of sight, she relaxed.

"Are you going to tell me now?" he asked. "Or am I wasting my time?"

She avoided his gaze and said nothing.

He turned off the music and cleaned up the area. "You did a great job today."

"Thank you," she said quietly.

He put on his shirt then walked with her to the door. "You might be sore tomorrow."

"Probably."

They walked outside then headed to his car. He opened the door and allowed her to get in first before he walked to his side.

"Wanna get some ice cream?" he asked as he placed his arm around her shoulders.

"I can't. I'm meeting Henry."

He nodded. "Do you know what you're going to say?"

"No," she said quietly.

"Good luck."

"Thanks."

"Are you going to tell him about me?"

"If he takes it well."

"I can tell you right now that he won't."

"I know." She wrapped her arm around his waist and leaned her head on his shoulder as he drove back to school. They didn't speak on the drive back. She was comfortable just holding him next to her, feeling safe. She never felt that way with anyone, that someone could protect her. It was the first time she wanted that.

When he parked the car, he looked at her. "I hate to say goodbye."

She pulled away and pressed her forehead against his. "Thank you for everything."

He kissed her on the forehead. "You don't need to thank me."

"But I do."

120

"You're the one doing all the work. I'm just guiding you."

"You do a lot more than that."

"You were strong when you came to me. I like making you stronger."

"Thank you."

"I really wish you would tell me."

"I wish you would stop asking me."

His eyes turned dark. "Do you not trust me?"

"Of course I do. I just don't want to talk about it."

"Fine."

"Please don't be angry with me."

"I'm not."

"It seems like you are."

"I'm frustrated."

"I'm sorry."

"It's okay." He grabbed her face and looked into her eyes. "I'll stop asking you."

"Thank you."

"But I'm here to listen whenever you're ready."

"I know," she said with a smile.

"Well, I guess this is it," he said sadly.

"Yeah."

He kissed her on the lips gently then pulled away. "I have to make it short. Otherwise, I'll take you in the backseat and never let you go."

"That doesn't sound so bad."

"Don't tempt me," he said as he rubbed his nose against hers. "Come on." He opened the door then helped her out. When he walked her to the Jeep, he kissed her on the head. "I'll see you tomorrow."

"Why did you come to me at lunch today?" she blurted.

He smiled. "Is that okay?"

"Yeah. But I wanted to keep this a secret."

"Did I make it obvious?"

"I don't think so."

"Well, I want to spend time with you even if it's just as your friend."

"I like spending time with you too."

"Plus, I don't want your friends to be totally shocked when they find out about us. At least this way, it will actually make sense."

"I suppose."

He kissed her again. "Goodnight, baby."

She smiled. "Goodnight."

He walked away and climbed back into his car. When she got inside her Jeep, she turned on the engine and drove home. She turned on the radio and thought about Coen, kissing his lips and running her fingers through his hair. That hour spent making out in the library was too short. She could do that all day.

When she pulled into her driveway, she saw Henry's car parked in front of the house. Her heart fell. She forgot about the death blow she was about to unleash. He was sitting on the front porch and stood up when she opened the car door. He was wearing jeans and sandals, and a thin shirt that showed the contours of his body. The time he spent at the gym every morning before school kept him firm and toned underneath his clothes.

"Hey," she said as he wrapped his arms around her, holding her to his chest. The touch definitely wasn't friendly.

He pulled away and glanced down to her body, seeing her breasts pushed up in her sports bra. She felt the heat of his gaze. "You look...sweaty."

"Yeah. I was just at the gym." She wasn't sure why she said that. It was pretty obvious.

"How was it?"

"It was okay." She walked to the front door and he walked beside her, his shoulder pressed against hers.

"What are you making for dinner?"

"What do you want?"

"I like everything you make."

She unlocked the door and they walked inside. Henry sat on the couch and Sydney immediately pulled on a sweater to hide her stomach and chest. She should have brought one to begin with. She didn't feel uncomfortable when Coen stared at her with obvious lust, but she didn't like the look from Henry. She felt like she was encouraging his obsession with her.

When she returned to the living room, she sat beside him.

He stared at her intently, a wide smile on his face. He was practically glowing with his own light. The happiness leaked out of his pores when he was with her. His glee was evident. "So what do you want to do? Watch a movie? Go for a swim?"

She placed her hands in her lap and squeezed them, taking a deep breath. "I wanted to talk to you about something."

The light of happiness disappeared. "What's wrong?" he said as he moved closer to her. "Are you okay?"

"I'm fine, Henry."

"Then what is it?"

She said nothing for a long time. It was harder than she thought it would be. She wished she could just ignore the situation and hope he'd get over his feelings on his own, but if he felt this way for two years, something needed to be said. She had to end his dream about them getting together if he was ever going to move on. As much as she hated it, she knew it had to be done. "I...I know about your feelings."

He shifted his weight, clearly uncomfortable. "Wha—what do you mean?"

"I know how you feel about me, Henry."

He swallowed the lump in his throat then looked away. "You do?" he whispered.

"Yeah."

He was quiet for a long time. "When did you find out?"

"The other day."

"What gave me away?"

"I just finally realized it. The way you look at me, the way you smile at me."

He sighed. "Well, I love being around you."

"And I love being around you."

He nodded. "I know."

It became awkward. The silence stretched between them for minutes.

"Do you feel the same way?"

She closed her eyes. "Henry—"

"I got it." He looked away and stared at the floor, trying to hide the obvious despair on his face. It was like the world had ended for him. Eternal night shined in his eyes, blocking out the sun and the light.

She grabbed his hand. "You're my best friend. I love you."

He squeezed it without looking at her. "I love you too."

"But I don't feel that way about you. I'm sorry."

He breathed heavily but said nothing. He stood up then walked out the front door, closing it behind him. She stared at the wall for a long time before she followed him. He wasn't outside when she stepped onto the dirt, but his car was still there. She knew where he was. She walked to the beach then sat down beside him. He wiped his tears away, staring straight ahead.

Seeing him cry made her cry. "Henry," she said as she wrapped her arms around him. "I'm so sorry."

He hugged her tightly, burying his face in her neck.

"I love you so much. I hate hurting you."

"It's okay," he said as he ran his hand down her back.

"I don't want to lose you," she whispered.

"Don't ever worry about that. You can't."

"I'm so sorry, Henry."

He hushed her. "It's okay."

When she pulled away, she saw the red line around his eyes. His eyes were still glossy with tears. She pressed her face against his and closed her eyes, trying to comfort him in any way that she could.

He pulled her into his lap and kept his face close to hers. "Give me a chance."

"What?"

"Go on a date with me. Just once."

"But...I don't feel that way about you."

"Because I've always been a friend to you. Let me take you out. We'll do the whole thing. Try seeing me as more than just a friend. I would treat you right, love you, and take care of you."

"Henry, I—"

"Please. Why not? We have nothing to lose. If you still don't feel anything, then we can forget about it and go back to being friends. Just give me a chance."

"I'm sorry."

"Why? What's wrong with me?"

"Not a single thing, Henry."

"Then why not?"

"I already told you I don't feel that way about you."

"I think you would if you let me take you out."

"Please don't make this harder for me."

He was quiet for a moment. "I wish I went for you to begin with instead of being your friend. Perhaps things would be different. But I'm not going to make that same mistake twice. If I want something, I need to seize it."

She said nothing.

"Can you just think about it?"

She already turned him down so many times. She couldn't do it anymore. "Okay."

"Thank you," he said as he hugged her.

She leaned on his shoulder and they watched the waves crash against the shore.

"I don't think you'll regret it," he said.

She tightened her jacket around her shoulders.

"You haven't been with anyone since Aaron and I know why." She sat up and looked at him. His eyes were still moist, but she saw the determination in them as well. His love was a beacon of light that shined brighter than the stars overhead. "Because you know you're supposed to be with me."

## 11

"Is everything going to change?" she asked as they walked to her front door.

"I hope not," he said as he placed his hands in his pockets.

"I'm so scared that I'm going to lose you."

He grabbed her arms. "That won't happen—not ever."

"Maybe you need some space right now. Are you going to be okay seeing me every day?"

"We'll see what happens after we have our date."

"I said I would think about it. I didn't agree to it."

He wrapped his arms around her waist and held her close. "If you want me to get on my knees and beg, I will." His soft words hung heavy in the air. "Just give me this. If it doesn't work out, I can move on. But not knowing what we could have been will kill me. Please."

"But I don't feel that way for you, Henry. I've said it so many times."

"And you might change your mind. I've said that many times." He released his hold on her. "We'll discuss it tomorrow." He looked down at the ground and avoided her gaze.

"Henry, I'm sorry things couldn't be different."

"I believe you."

"Well, goodnight."

"Yeah," he said with a sad voice. He turned around and walked back to his car. The obvious slump of his shoulders and the slow movement of his legs told Sydney everything she needed to know. He was completely heartbroken over her rejection. She hated seeing him in pain, but she didn't know what else to do.

He got inside his car then drove away without looking at her. She stood on her front porch for a long time, listening to the waves in the distance and the crickets rubbing their legs together. She feared that she would lose their friendship eventually, especially after he found out about Coen. When the tears started to fall, she sat down on the stairs and held herself. The grief wouldn't stop. She automatically pulled out her phone and called Coen even though she didn't know what she would say.

"Is everything okay, baby?" he asked with a deep voice. She could tell that he just woke up by his deep breathing. He sighed deeply as his mind started to awaken.

"No," she whispered through her tears.

"It didn't go well, I take it?"

She said nothing.

"I'm on my way."

"Okay."

She stayed on the phone and heard him change then grab his keys. When she heard the sound of an engine, she knew he was on his way. They said nothing as he drove to her house, just listening to each other breathe. She kept her whimpers to a minimum because she hated crying. It was weak and pathetic.

When he pulled up to the dirt road, they still didn't hang up. He parked the car then shut the door behind him. The phone was still pressed to his ear as he walked toward her. He was wearing a shirt that had the sleeves cut off and running shorts. Even though he was in sleepwear, he looked sexy. His hair was messy, sticking out everywhere, and his eyes were slightly droopy. His arms moved slightly as he walked toward her, showing the definition of his muscles. When he reached her, he hung up then slid the phone into his pocket along with his keys.

"Hey," she whispered.

He kneeled down in front of her. "Let's lay down."

"Okay," she said weakly.

He grabbed her hands and pulled her to a stand. He followed as she walked inside and they headed to her bedroom. Even though they were going into her room, she didn't feel uncomfortable being so intimate with him. It felt right.

He shut the door behind him and took off his shirt then his shorts, standing in his boxers.

Sydney was too depressed to feel lustful toward him, but she did notice the lines of his stomach and his small hips. He reached her and unbuttoned her jeans then pulled them off, leaving her standing in her underwear. He pulled her shirt off then stared at her for a moment, desire shining in his eyes.

"Beautiful," he whispered.

She grabbed his shirt from the floor. "Can I wear this?"

He smiled. "Why?"

"It smells like you."

"I'll be lying right next to you."

"I still want to."

"Keep it," he said as he kissed her on the head.

"Really?"

"It's yours."

He walked to the bed then got under the covers. She had a queen sized bed that sat in the center of the room. The wooden headboard contrasted against the white color of the walls. When he lay down, the bed looked small because he took up most of it. He was much taller and bigger than she was. With him, she felt tiny.

He patted the bed. "Come on."

She crawled beside him and wrapped her arm around his stomach, her head resting on his wide chest. He was warm and soft. She could lie there for days and never move.

His hand ran through her hair. "So, what happened?"

"He was crushed."

"I don't blame him."

"He cried."

"I'm sorry."

"I hate hurting him. It just completely cripples me."

"I know," he said as he continued to comb his fingers through her hair. "It's not your fault. You didn't know."

"I should have."

"You only see what you want to see in people. And you don't realize how beautiful you are."

She said nothing to his comment.

"Is your friendship over?"

"He said I'll never lose him as a friend."

"That's good. The hardest part is over. Now he just has to move on. It's better this way."

She sighed. "He asked if I would go on a date with him just to see if I could feel something for him."

Coen's hand stiffened. "And what did you say?"

"I would think about it."

He sat up, pushing her from his chest. "Why would you say that?" His eyes flashed in anger as he looked at her.

"He begged me to. He said that he just wants a single opportunity. Nothing is going to happen. I was just trying to humor him."

"If he takes you out on date, he's going to touch you, woo you, and kiss you at the end of the night. This better be a fucking joke."

She sat up and looked at him, feeling his light shirt against her skin. "Nothing would happen. I wouldn't let him kiss me."

"It doesn't matter. I'm your boyfriend. He isn't. How would you feel if I went on a date with someone? Even if I didn't plan on kissing her?" She didn't like that idea at all. "You can be best friends with him, hang out alone, do whatever you want because I trust you, but this is unacceptable. You go on a date with him, we're done."

She stared at him, seeing the certainty in his eyes. There was no point in arguing with him. He had a valid point.

"I'm already your closet boyfriend, which I can't stand, but I refuse to let this happen. So what's it going to be?"

She leaned in and kissed his lips gently. "You're right. I'll tell him no tomorrow."

He took a deep breath. "Thank you."

"I wouldn't want you to go on a date with someone else."

"It will just give him false hope, Sydney. Even if he begs you, you have to be strong. It isn't going to happen. He needs to move on. I know it's painful, but you're just making this harder for him."

"I know."

He kissed her on the forehead. "Thank you. I thought I was going to have to spend all night trying to convince you. I can tell you have a hard head."

"I'm stubborn when I believe in my decision. When you explained your feelings about it, I understood. You've been very patient and understanding of this entire ordeal."

"Very patient," he said with a smile. "I really want to sit next to you in class, walk you to your next period, hold your hand during lunch, and kiss you whenever I fucking feel like it."

"Me too."

"Henry is going to find out eventually. Just tell him the truth. It will be painful, but it will help him move on. When he sees you with me, he'll know that I make you happy."

"No. I can't do that. Give him some time."

He sighed in frustration.

"I'm sorry."

"I meant what I said. I won't put up with this for long. I hate being a secret."

"That's fine. I don't want you to be a secret either."

"Okay." He lay down and cradled her to his chest. "Thank you for calling me."

"Thank you for coming."

"I'll always come."

She hugged him tightly, feeling the muscles over his ribs. "You make me feel safe. I've never felt that way before."

He ran his fingers through her hair. He said nothing for a long time. She knew he was thinking about her unknown attacker. She waited for him to ask who the culprit was, but he never did, just like he promised. She didn't want to tell him the truth but a part of her did. She would confess her secret eventually. It was just too depressing to discuss it now.

"I will protect you with my life, Sydney. But I suspect you won't ever need me. You're almost as strong as I am."

"I need you in other ways."

"I like knowing that I make you feel safe."

"Me too," she whispered. She ran her hand along his forearm and looked at his tattoo. "What does this mean?"

He turned his forearm in her grasp. "My tat?"

She nodded.

"My dog passed away and I wanted to honor him."

"Your dog?"

"His name was Brutus. I had him for sixteen years. He was my best friend. We grew up together. Whenever I did my homework, he sat beside me. When I came home late at night, he always sat on the porch, waiting for me. When I cried because my parents said I had to go to this horrible daycare, he licked my tears away. I miss him."

"I'm so sorry, Coen."

"It's okay. He had a long and happy life. I just miss him sometimes."

She ran her fingers over the marking. "Why is it drawn as a wolf or beast—a wild dog?"

He smiled. "He always acted tougher than he really was. He chased down dogs, fought large rodents, barked at me when I didn't feed him quick enough, and even chewed tires off cars. And he was huge, not fat, just big. It was like living with a wild wolf. That's how I remember him—a ferocious beast."

His words brought tears to her eyes. When she saw the tattoo, she assumed it was something lame and stupid. She automatically judged him for it when she shouldn't have. He was unbelievably sensitive and sweet. "I'm sorry, Coen."

"I know," he said as he kissed her tears away. "You don't need to cry."

"I can't help it. I...I hate thinking about you being in pain."

"It was hard for a while—the first year. Whenever I saw his feeding bowls, I started to feel the tears form. Sometimes I thought I heard his growl when he wasn't really there. I would wake up in the middle of the night to let him out, but then I remembered he was gone. And the dreams—those always made me cry." He paused for a second. "But now when I think about him every day, it doesn't hurt as much. I think about all the funny or the stupid things he did. I still miss him, but now his memories make me smile. So please don't feel sad for me. I hate it when you do that."

"I can't help it," she whispered.

"You carry the weight of everyone's grief on your shoulders. You shouldn't. Things happen, hearts are broken, but you can't let it break you down like this."

She knew he was talking about Henry as well as himself. "It's hard not to."

He turned on his side and cupped her cheek. "I love that about you, but I hate seeing you sad."

"I know how you feel."

He grabbed his phone. "Would you like to see pictures?"

She smiled. "Of course."

He showed her some pictures on his phone. Brutus was massive just like he said he was. There were pictures of him in the back of the truck or sitting on the floor.

"He was very cute."

He laughed. "He knew he was too. That guy got anything he wanted out of me. I used to make him turkey omelets for breakfast."

"Well, now I know why he was so fat."

"He wasn't fat—just muscular."

"Uh, Coen. He was just fat."

"No."

She smiled at him. "I hate to break it to you."

He shook his head. "He was just big boned and furry."

"Whatever you say."

He put his phone back on the nightstand. "Did you have any pets?"

"I have a lot of pets."

"Now?"

She nodded.

"Where are they?"

"In the ocean. The aquarium. The trees."

He smiled. "You're such a hippy."

"I'll take that as a compliment. One of my pets is a dolphin. Her name is Rose."

"Is she fat?" he teased.

"Dolphins can't be fat."

"They might."

"It isn't possible."

"I'll have to see for myself."

"You wanna? I can show you."

"Any friend of yours is a friend of mine," he said as he rubbed his nose against hers.

Looking into his eyes made her melt. The moon shined through the window and highlighted the blue color of his irises. "Your eyes remind me of the ocean."

"Thank you."

"They're beautiful."

"Not as beautiful as you. You know what I see when I look into yours?"

"What?"

"The forest, the birds, the butterflies—nature. I see everything that is beautiful in the world. The blades of grass that line the ground, the fallen branches from trees, the grasshoppers that hide in the leaves. I see everything in you."

Her eyes stung with tears. Nothing so beautiful had ever been said to her. "Coen—"

He kissed her. "I mean it."

"I know."

"You're different than other girls. I really like you. You're everything that I ever wanted in another person."

"Really?"

"No. You are much more."

She ran her fingers through his hair. "When I first saw you, I just wanted to sleep with you. You're so sexy and fine. I fantasized about you being naked, lying on top of me. I even had a sex dream about you that made me come harder than I ever have. But now I see so much more in you, something I never imagined. You're amazing, Coen. Nothing like what I expected."

"I'm glad that you realize there's more to me than sex. You aren't like the rest of them, the girls that thought the same thing."

"Did Audrey love you?"

He flinched. "I hate talking about her. I don't think about her anymore."

"I didn't mean to upset you," she whispered.

"No. She never did. She liked having me around, a man on her arm. She never listened to anything I said. When I told her about Brutus, she just laughed. The only connection we ever really had was when we were in the bedroom—and that's because we weren't talking."

"She's stupid."

"Yeah, definitely."

"Are you still friends?"

"No."

"Then why do I still see you with her?"

He sighed. "I'm only answering your questions so you understand that I have no feelings for her whatsoever."

"That's not why I'm asking. I just want to know you better."

"She wants me back. She's wanted me back for a long time."

"And your rejection isn't enough?"

"No. I took her back once. She hopes that I'll do it again."

Sydney ran her fingers through his hair but said nothing.

"Which is why I want to make our relationship public. She'll finally leave me alone."

"You know I can't do that right now."

"Then I'll have to keep avoiding her as much as possible."

"I'm sorry."

"It's okay."

"Was she your first?"

"No. Was Aaron yours?"

"Yes."

"So I would be your second?"

She nodded.

"You must have really loved him, then."

"I thought I did."

"He's an idiot. You're better off with me anyway."

She smiled. "I know I am."

"Am I going to have to deal with him when we tell everyone?" Coen asked, his hand gliding down her neck and to her shoulder.

"He isn't like that. He's actually a very sweet guy."

"Well, that's a relief."

"I think Henry will be a bigger problem." Sydney didn't want to think about that. Every time she did it made her miserable.

"I don't think so."

"He'll be totally crushed."

Coen placed his hand on her cheek. "But he won't interfere with our relationship. That guy loves you irrevocably, Sydney. I know he wants you to be happy even if it isn't with him."

"How could you possibly know that?"

"I've seen him with you every day. He watches everything you do, puts you before himself in every way, even if it is just by opening a door. That guy would take a knife to the chest just to spare you any pain. He's a good guy—I can tell. But he'll back off once he knows the truth, which is why I think you should tell him."

She sighed. "Let's give him some time to adjust."

"I love how selfless you are, but at a certain point, you have to take care of yourself first. Henry wants you to be happy. Right now, you aren't."

"I love him. I'll do whatever I can to make this easier for him."

"Nothing will make this easy. There's no optimal choice when handling this situation. What if I talk to him?"

"Absolutely not. It has to come from me."

"Okay." He ran his hands up her side and rested his fingers on the skin of her ribs. "We'll play this out however you wish."

"Thank you."

"Okay. It's time for bed," he said as he moved closer to her. "Go to sleep."

She ran her hand across his chest and felt his shoulders. "I'm not tired."

"Neither am I."

"Then...why don't we do something?"

"What did you have in mind?"

"Fooling around."

He sighed. "I don't trust myself with you. You make me feel things I can't even explain. I think it's best if we don't. We're lying together practically naked in a bed. It might get out of control."

"I promise it won't."

He stared at her. "Last time, you asked me to fuck you, which I almost did."

"But you didn't. You kept your word to me. I'll keep mine to you."

"As tempting as that sounds, my answer is still no."

"Please."

He closed his eyes. "I love hearing you say that word."

She ran her fingers through his hair. "Just kissing and touching each other over our clothes."

"What clothes? We're not wearing anything."

"I promise," she whispered.

He was quiet for a moment. "I'm trusting you."

"And it's well placed."

"Okay."

He leaned in and sealed his lips over hers, kissing her gently. The sound of their caressing lips filled her ears and made her shake. When he slipped his tongue inside, she fisted his hair, loving his taste. She pulled him on top of her. When she wrapped her legs around his waist, he ran his hands up her thigh, feeling the delicate skin.

His hard cock pressed against her as he leaned over her. The front of his boxers was just as wet as her

138

underwear. When he rocked into her, she felt him rub against her clit, making her gasp into his mouth. Just the gentle touch was enough to start the formation of an orgasm, which hovered in the back of her mind.

She slipped her hands down his back, scratching the surface of his skin as she went. When he moved against her, he moaned, breathing into her mouth.

"I'm officially gone," he said against her mouth.

"Good."

He kissed her harder while rubbing against her.

She knew she was the only somewhat logical person at that moment. If she asked him to fuck her, he would. She promised to remain in control so she did, letting him enjoy the moment between them without any guilt or stress, just as he had done to her.

He gripped her hips and pushed against her harder.

"Coen," she said with a gasp. He was going to make her come like that. Just feeling his dick against her was enough to make her explode. They were dry humping like teenagers, but she felt more aroused than she did when she and Aaron had sex. Coen was different than anyone she had ever met. There was a connection between them that she could never explain.

"Let me inside you," he whispered. "I want to feel you."

She kissed him and cut off his words, running her fingers through his hair. When he rubbed against her again, she felt the walls break down. It started off slow and intense, crashing through her until it burst into a fiery ball of flame. She gripped him tightly as her entire body tensed, and she felt the pleasure roll through her like the tide during the rise of the moon. It felt so good that she was dizzy. Her lips became immobile as she enjoyed it, breathing into his mouth with loud gasps and moans. She got louder but was unable to stop herself. He stopped kissing her and just listened to her sounds, becoming harder because she was coming for him. When she was finished, she gripped him tightly, not wanting it to end.

Coen pulled down his boxers, but she steadied his hands, knowing what he was going to do. "No."

"I don't want to come in my underwear," he said. "That's all."

She released the rim of his shorts and let him pull them down. He pressed his cock directly against her wet clitoris and rubbed against her. He didn't kiss her, but looked into her eyes as he gently slid across her skin. She gripped the back of his neck and moved with him, increasing the friction and stimulation. When he started to breathe heavily, his muscles tightening under her, she knew he was about to come. With a loud gasp, he came on top of her, moaning the entire time. His eyes never left hers as the pleasure shot through him.

When he was finished, he kissed her gently. "I haven't done that since high school but I really enjoyed it."

"I did too."

"I'm glad I can make you come so easily."

"Well, look at you. It isn't difficult to do."

He smiled. "I like what I'm hearing."

She ran her hands up his back then cupped his face, kissing him gently. His lips responded to her touch and he caressed her, feeling her lips intently. Her heart ached when she felt him, not from pain, but from joy. It was so strong, it was frightening. When she looked into his eyes, she saw the same expression. The trust between them was unshakeable, and the adoration they felt for one another was unbreakable. She had never felt that way in her entire life, not with her family, friends, or significant others. This was different in every way.

He kissed her on the forehead. "I'm going to get a towel." He rose from the bed then walked away, leaving her paralyzed with emotion. When he returned, he wiped the mess away. "Sorry about that."

"I like it."

"You do?"

"It's hot."

"At least I don't feel so disgusting now."

She grabbed his arm and pulled him to bed. "Definitely not disgusting."

He turned on his side and draped his hand over her. "I can't keep my eyes open," he said as he sighed.

She kissed him on the forehead. "Goodnight. You deserve a long rest."

He growled. "I don't even want to know what time it is."

She glanced at the clock but didn't reveal the time. "Goodnight."

"Hmm."

She pressed her forehead against his and listened to his breathing before she fell asleep. The slow cadence of his heartbeat and his breaths made her forget about every bad thing that ever happened to her. She forgot about Henry, her family, her job—everything. It was just them against the world.

# 12

Coen woke up when the alarm went off then took off to his place to shower. Seeing him go made her heart throb. Being apart from him was pure torture. She knew she had to keep their relationship a secret for Henry's sake, but she really hated it. She hated seeing Coen sit across the classroom, not even acknowledging her. She wanted the whole world to know that they were together.

When she saw Henry in the parking lot that morning, she felt her stomach convulse in nausea. She knew what he wanted to discuss.

When he reached her, he looked at her. "How about tonight?"

"Henry, I thought about it and I really think it's a bad idea."

He sighed. "Why?"

"I just feel like I would be leading you on."

"But—"

"I'm not going to change my mind."

He looked wounded by her interruption.

"Henry, do you really want to be with me if it's forced? Don't you want it to be natural?"

"I don't care how it is. I just want to be with you. It really doesn't matter if you don't love me nearly as much as I love you. You'll get there eventually."

She looked over his shoulder and saw Coen walk down the sidewalk toward them. He stared at her but his expression was stoic. "Henry, that is my final answer. No."

He bowed his head, running his hands over his face. "Okay."

"I'm sorry."

He said nothing.

Coen stopped when he reached them. "I heard we have a quiz today."

Henry looked away and stared at the building, hiding his face. He was on the verge of tears and Sydney knew it. She saw his chest expand with heightened breaths and his eyes flutter with accumulated tears.

"We'll see you in class, Coen," she said without looking at him.

He looked at her for a moment. "Okay." He walked away without looking back. She knew he was just trying to give her the courage to be strong.

Henry shifted his weight then ran his fingers through his hair. The pain was etched into every line of his face. "I'll...I'll catch you later," he said as he turned around.

She grabbed him and held him in her arms. "It's okay, Henry."

"I need space."

"It's going to be okay," she said. "You're going to find someone that you love way more than you love me."

"But I only love you." His voice shook with emotion.

"For now."

He rested his head on top of hers. Their first class had already started but she couldn't leave Henry. She never missed a class but he was more important than perfect attendance.

"I'm sorry that I'm acting like this," he whispered.

"Please don't apologize."

"I'm not usually an emotional guy."

"I know you aren't. Please don't explain yourself."

After a moment, he composed himself. "You should get to class."

"*We* should get to class."

He shook his head. "I'm going to head home."

"Where you go, I go," she said as she grabbed his hand. "Now, let's go to class."

He said nothing.

"Let's get back to normal. We don't need to talk about this anymore. Fake it until you make it, Henry."

"Okay."

She smiled. "Let's go." She held his hand as they walked to the science building, caressing his knuckles. When they got inside, she dropped his hand. Professor Jones looked at Sydney as she moved to her seat but he continued to lecture. Coen had his eyes glued to her face, making sure she was okay.

They sat down next to Nancy, who looked at them with a heightened eyebrow.

"Is everything okay?" she whispered to Sydney.

"We're fine," she whispered back. She took out her notebook and started to scribble away. When she glanced at Henry, he was leaning back in his chair, staring at the surface of the table. He wasn't looking at the board or listening to the lecture. He looked completely miserable.

Sydney sighed then returned to her notes. She would have done anything to make this easier on Henry but she didn't know what. Like the common cold, she had to wait for Henry to defeat it on his own.

When the class was over, they walked to their next period, which Henry was equally depressed in. Sydney wouldn't let herself look at him because she wanted to cry every time she did. She wished she could give him what he wanted just so he would be happy, but she couldn't do that. Coen was her boyfriend, the person she really wanted. He made her feel things that were completely alien to her. The night before, she felt something burst in her chest when they kissed and touched. It was one of the greatest nights of her life, but also the worst.

They went to their usual table in the cafeteria when lunchtime arrived. Nancy was already there, reading through her notes. She looked at them both when they sat down.

Sydney glared at Nancy, silently asking her not to ask what was wrong. She could read her mind.

"Hi," Nancy said awkwardly.

Henry said nothing.

"They have lasagna for lunch today," Sydney said to Henry. It was his favorite.

He shrugged. "I'm not hungry right now."

She sighed, defeated, then turned to her textbook. Henry sat across from her with his arms over his chest, staring outside the window. His mind was elsewhere, probably thinking about Sydney.

Nancy looked across the room. "Is he gonna have lunch with us again?"

Sydney assumed she meant Coen. When she followed her gaze, she saw him approach the table. He took the seat right next to Sydney.

"What's up," he said as he sat down. He placed a chicken salad on the table and started to eat, acting like everything was totally platonic. The electricity that buzzed between them was heavy in the air. If she felt it, he must have felt it too. When she thought about what they did the night before, she squeezed her thighs together. Arousal coursed through her and she felt awkward. She was worried that everyone knew what she was thinking about.

When Coen smiled at her, she knew he recognized her thoughts. "Hi."

"Oh. Hi," she stuttered.

"Class was interesting," he said.

"I liked it," she answered.

He ate his salad, practically inhaling it, then wiped his face with a napkin.

She was surprised he chose a salad. It wasn't very masculine. "You like salads?"

"They're good."

"You aren't still hungry?"

"I had a big breakfast."

Nancy eyed him suspiciously. "Are you having lunch with us every day now?"

"As long as I'm welcome."

Nancy started to twirl her hair around her finger, becoming playful. "Yeah?"

Sydney recognized that look. Nancy thought Coen was visiting her, not Sydney.

Coen leaned back. "I like seeing Sydney outside the study room."

She knew that was his way of declaring his interest for her without being too blunt about it. They had to be careful if they wanted to preserve their secret.

"Why? Sydney is boring."

"Hey," Sydney said, offended.

"Well, I think she's interesting," Coen said in her defense.

Henry still looked out the window, ignoring their conversation entirely. Sydney wasn't sure if he even noticed Coen's presence.

Coen positioned himself in his seat so he was facing Sydney more than he was facing Nancy, a delicate way of rejecting her. Sydney really wished they could just be honest, but when she looked at Henry, she knew she couldn't do that. He was totally miserable.

"So, same time and place?" he asked.

"Yeah."

He nodded. "Thanks for helping me. I feel like I really understand the material now."

She blushed, unable to control it. "You're welcome."

He stared at her like she was the only person in the room.

"Coen?"

He turned around and looked at the blonde that approached the table. "Oh. Hi," he said sadly.

She placed her hand on her hip then eyed the group with disdain, her glare lingering on Sydney a little longer than on everyone else. "Come over to us," she said as she nodded to her table, which was a group of pretty women that looked like cheerleaders.

"No, thanks, Audrey."

She grabbed his arm but he pulled it away. "Stop being silly."

"I'm not," he snapped. "I'm hanging out with my friends. Please leave me alone."

"These aren't your friends," she spat. "What about John, Ted, and Michael?"

Sydney noticed how they were all guys.

"I can have more than three friends," he snapped.

Sydney was surprised by the venom in his voice. She had never heard him sound so angry. He was practically livid.

She smiled then leaned toward him, her lips moving toward his. He leaned back and grabbed her arm. "You're just embarrassing yourself right now."

"Stop treating your girlfriend like that."

"You aren't my girlfriend."

"Yes, I am," she said as she crossed her arms over her chest. "I know it can't be one of these two girls."

"I think they are both gorgeous," he snapped.

"Well, she isn't," she said as she looked at Sydney.

Sydney tried not to let the insult bother her but it did.

Coen stood up at the same time Henry did. Sydney knew Audrey crossed a line with both of them.

Sydney grabbed his hand. "Let it go."

Coen stared at her for a long time, silently communicating with her. He wanted to tell Audrey that Sydney was his girlfriend, but she wasn't ready for that, not with Henry standing so close by. He looked at Audrey. "Don't talk about my friend like that."

Henry marched up to her, anger etched on his face. Henry didn't get mad very often. Only when something catastrophic happened. "Take your fake tits and get the fuck away from her," he snapped, his eyes wide.

Sydney was shocked by the words that flew from this mouth. Henry never spoke like that—at least she thought he didn't.

Audrey glared at them both before she walked away.

Henry watched her leave before he returned to his seat. Coen sat down and said nothing for a long time.

Sydney looked at them both. "I appreciate you both standing up for me, but it's unnecessary. Her insults say more about her than they do about me."

Coen stared at her, incredulous. "You're amazing."

Nancy eyed them both when she heard him.

Sydney looked away and tried to dissipate the obvious chemistry between them. If Nancy and Henry didn't notice it, they were both blind. She looked at Henry. "Please don't talk like that again."

"I'm sorry," he said. "It just came out."

She stared at him, still surprised by his unexpected ferocity.

"I was just upset," he whispered. "It won't happen again."

She breathed a sigh of relief. Getting Henry expelled would just make her life more difficult.

Coen looked at them all. "I apologize for that."

"Your girlfriend is a bitch," Nancy said.

"She isn't my girlfriend," he said quickly. "But you're right. She is a fucking bitch."

"She seems to think there's something between you," Nancy pressed.

"Well, there isn't," he snapped. He grabbed his backpack then stood up. "I'll see you later." He left the cafeteria from the door on the other side of the room so he could avoid his psycho ex.

Sydney went to lab with Henry, but he wasn't responsive through the whole period. She did the entire experiment by herself while he watched, his face stoic. She didn't berate him for being a bad lab partner. She knew his heart was broken, shattered into a million pieces. Hopefully, he would get better soon.

After class was over, Henry walked with her outside. "I guess I'll see you around," he said sadly.

"Henry?"

"What?"

"I'm here for you."

"I know."

"Call me if you need me."

"I need you all the time, Sydney. But you can't help me."

"I wish I could."

"Whoever you end up with is the luckiest guy in the world."

She felt the tears spring from her eyes. "Thank you. And whoever you end up with is the luckiest girl in the world."

He said nothing then walked away.

After she watched him leave the parking lot, she walked to the library and entered the study room. The curtain was pulled down over the window, so she knew Coen wanted to have another make out session.

She placed her backpack on the table then sat beside him.

His eyes were dark when he looked at her. "Please don't leave me."

"Why would I?"

He bowed his head. "Because of Audrey."

"I don't care about her."

"I'm so sorry about this afternoon. I would tell her the truth—that I'm happy and committed to you, but I know you don't want that."

"You handled the situation as best you could."

"I know psycho ex-girlfriends are a huge turn off. I just don't want her rudeness and bitchiness to scare you off."

She placed her hand on his. "Please don't worry about that."

He breathed a sigh of relief. "Thank god."

"I'm not going anywhere. You can calm down now."

"Okay. But you don't deserve that."

"She'll back off when she knows we're together. I doubt she's going to bother me again."

"She better not. Otherwise, I'll make her regret it."

"That's not funny."

"I wasn't trying to be." His eyes shined with determination. "I don't want you to be harassed. It's unacceptable."

"I can take care of myself. You know I can."

He smiled. "That's true."

"Now forget about it, okay?"

"It's forgotten."

"So, another make out session?"

"Come here." He pulled her onto his lap and started to kiss her passionately. Their kisses usually started out gentle, but his embrace was intense from the beginning. She didn't mind it in the least. His tongue felt wonderful against her mouth.

"I could kiss you all day," he said as he breathed into her mouth.

"I would love that."

His hands moved up her shirt and squeezed her breasts, making her even more excited. She didn't touch him in a more sexual way because they were in the library.

They would probably never get caught but it was still best to avoid anything too scandalous. After an hour went by, Coen pulled away.

"Do you have ChapStick?"

"I have some in my purse," she said as she rubbed his chest.

"Good. I'm in desperate need of it."

"Come over to my house."

He rubbed his nose against hers. "I have to work."

"You get off sometime."

"Then, I'm having dinner with my family."

"And what about after that?"

"Then I'm yours," he said with a smile.

"Good. I want to feel your body against mine."

He cupped her face. "We're taking this slow. Remember?"

"I know."

"Just don't forget."

"I'll try." She rose from his lap then handed him the ChapStick. He smeared it on then grabbed his backpack.

"Let's go."

They walked to their cars in the parking lot, not touching each other.

"I'll see you later, baby," he said as he put his hands in his pockets and looked at her.

"I look forward to it."

He rocked on his heels as he looked around, seeing if anyone was watching. "Fuck this," he said as he grabbed her face and pushed her against her Jeep. He kissed her while running his hands over her body, feeling her rounded hips and her flat stomach. She returned his affection with equal intensity, risking the chance of being spotted, but she didn't care at the moment. He kissed her neck then pulled away. "Now I can say goodbye."

"Bye."

"Now get in your car so I can't rape you."

"You can't rape the willing."

He growled. "Don't even go there." He grabbed her ass and pushed her into the seat. "I'll see you in a few hours."

"Okay." She started her Jeep then drove back to her house. She sat on the couch and waited anxiously for Coen to get there. When she wasn't with him, she missed him like crazy.

# 13

After Coen changed into his workout clothes, he went into the studio and waited for his client. He didn't check the paperwork because people always lied on their application about everything. Their height, weight, medical condition—everything. It was better if he saw them in person so he wouldn't be biased about them. He kept his shirt on because he didn't want to show his body to anyone now that he had a girlfriend. It was an effective way to motivate people and intimidate them, but he felt uncomfortable now that he was in a relationship. He wouldn't want other men staring at Sydney with lustful eyes. He respected her too much to do that.

When the door opened, he turned around.

"Hey, Coen," she said with a smile.

"Audrey?"

"I thought you could teach me some basics." She strolled over to him, rolling her hips. She wore spandex shorts that were practically underwear and a sports bra that pushed up her cleavage. Her hair cascaded over her shoulders. She looked like she was about to do a photo shoot, not a workout.

He was immediately annoyed. "I'm not training you."

"Too bad. I already paid."

"I'll reimburse you for it."

"No," she said as she stood in front of him. "Train me."

"Fuck you," he snapped.

Her eyes widened. "Do you want me to tell your boss how you're acting? You want to get fired?"

"Do you always threaten people you profess to love? Go ahead and tell him. I would rather lose my job than spend an hour with you."

She crossed her arms over her chest. "Do you have a thing for that ugly girl, Sydney?"

He raised an eyebrow. "I don't know an ugly girl named Sydney."

"That girl you had lunch with."

"I know a Sydney that's beautiful—on the inside as well as the outside."

"Are you into her?"

"Does it matter?"

"Well, you're supposed to be with me."

"I thought the same thing when you fucked that other guy."

"Would you stop throwing that in my face?"

"No. We're over—done."

"You gave me a second chance before. Why aren't you giving me another one now?"

"Because my feelings for you are gone."

"Impossible."

He laughed. "You're really full of yourself, aren't you?"

"You haven't been sleeping around."

"And how would you know that?"

"You haven't been going out."

He didn't comment to her statement.

"Because you can't get over me. I'm the best sex you've ever had, I'm the girl that your parents love, and I'm the only one who can understand your pain. I was there for you when Elaine died. Face it, I'm the one," she said as she stepped toward him, pressing her breasts against his chest.

He stepped away from her, putting distance between them. "I can't stand you, Audrey."

"You love me."

"I did love you. Not anymore. I'm over you."

"Who are you trying to fool?"

He shook his head. "Just go, Audrey."

"No."

He leaned against the wall. "Then we are just going to stand here for an hour while I ignore you."

"You won't train me because you don't trust yourself with me. You still want me."

"No. I can't stand you so the idea of touching you repulses me."

"Liar."

He looked away. "If you have any respect for me, you'll leave me alone."

"I love you and I'm not giving up on you."

"If you love me, you'll let me go," he snapped.

"This isn't over until I say it's over."

"Fuck you," he snapped. "You're fucking crazy." He grabbed his bag from the floor then walked toward the door.

"Where do you think you're going?" she said as she followed him.

"Away from you." He burst through the doors and walked to the front desk, looking at the man behind the counter. "My client has asthma. I can't train her."

He raised an eyebrow. "She does? Her paper says she doesn't."

"Well, she lied." When she reached him, he grabbed her bag and pulled the inhaler out. "There you go. I can't train her."

The worker looked at Audrey in disapproval. "Lying on your application makes you unqualified to receive specialized training. I'm sorry."

She glared at Coen with hatred. He smiled back before walking away. She followed him to his car.

"Stop walking away from me," she said as she chased him.

"Then stop following me." When he reached his car, she grabbed him, pinning him against the door.

"You aren't going anywhere." She pressed her breasts against his chest, trying to seduce him. Her lips were near his.

He smiled at her the whole time. "I'm as soft as a wet fish." He pushed her away then got into the car, turning on the engine while ignoring her. He pulled out of the parking lot without looking at her and drove to his parents' house near the base of the mountains.

He shook Audrey from his mind and focused on Sydney. When he thought about what they did the night before, it raised his sail. He wasn't attracted to anyone in the way he was attracted to her. He missed having sex on a regular basis but he would wait until she was ready. He wanted a relationship with her, not a short term fling. Also, he was afraid to give himself to her because he couldn't stand to lose her. He wanted to be there the next morning, sharing breakfast with her at the table. He was in this for the long haul. She was amazing and he wasn't going to let her go. Audrey was hideous in comparison to Sydney.

When he arrived at the house, he walked inside without knocking then joined his family at the dinner table. His brother, Jordan, was already seated next to their dad. They were two years apart and Jordan was in his freshman year at the university. He still lived at home.

"Hey," Coen said as he sat down.

His father nodded to him. "You're off work early."

"My client had asthma. I had to cut it short."

His mother placed the food on the table. "Well, that worked out. We were too hungry to wait."

His Uncle Gilbert looked at him. "How is the tutoring going?"

"Good. I aced the quiz today."

Coen's father nodded. "I'm glad my money isn't being wasted."

Coen said nothing. It definitely wasn't being wasted. "Uncle, I heard you have a research exhibition you are going on."

"Yes, in just a few weeks."

"Need any help?"

"Would you be interested?" he asked in surprise.

"No. But I know someone who would be a great asset to you."

He shook his head. "I hate undergraduates. They're totally clueless."

"Uh, thanks," Coen said with a laugh. "But this girl is wicked smart. You won't regret it."

"I'll pass, Coen."

"Please? She really wants to be a part of it. Just let her watch. That's all."

He smiled. "So this girl is really pretty, huh?"

He rolled his eyes. "That isn't why I'm recommending her."

"But she is, isn't she?"

"She's drop dead gorgeous."

"That's what I thought," he said with a laugh.

"Come on, Uncle. Do this as a favor to me."

"If you're failing your zoology class, I doubt you know any smart people."

"She's my tutor."

"I don't know anything about the girl. She'll probably just get in the way."

"You do know her. She works as a custodian at the aquarium."

He was quiet for a moment. "Stacy?"

"Sydney," he corrected.

"I don't know," he said hesitantly.

"I'll mow your lawn and do housework for a month if you just take her with you."

He raised an eyebrow. "Wow. Someone's in love."

Coen ignored his comment.

"So Audrey is history?" his uncle said.

"She's been history," Coen said. "So, will you take her?"

"You've got yourself a deal," he said as he shook Coen's hand.

Coen nodded, pleased that he could do this for Sydney. "And invite her yourself. Don't tell her I asked you to."

"Got it."

Coen smiled, happy that he got Sydney a position on the boat. He knew how much she wanted it. Also, he knew his uncle would be happy that she was there once he got to know her.

During dinner, they talked about school and work. Coen focused on eating his food and stayed out of the conversation. His mind was on Sydney. When he finally left, he went by his apartment and changed before he parked in front of her house.

When he got out, he saw her sprinting toward him with a smile on her face. She jumped into his arms and started to kiss him passionately, gripping his shoulders. His heart melted. It was a moment he would remember forever. Seeing the bright look on her face when she saw him was priceless.

"You missed me?" he asked as he put her down.

"So much."

"How did you know I was here?"

"I've been looking out the window like an obsessed teenager."

"That's adorable," he said as he kissed her on the head. "Wanna get some ice cream?"

"I like ice cream."

"Good." He opened the passenger door for her. "Let's go."

He came around the other side and sat beside her.

She wrapped her arm around his and placed her hand on his thigh, leaning against him. "How was your day?"

He was quiet for a moment. The incident with Audrey immediately came to his mind. It wasn't something worth mentioning but he felt like a liar if he didn't. He wasn't a liar and hated being deceitful. It wasn't in his nature. "Audrey was my client today."

"What? You trained her?"

"I asked her to leave and when she didn't, I told my colleague that she had asthma so I wouldn't have to train her."

"So she was trying to get you back the whole time?"

He sighed. "Unfortunately."

She said nothing, unsure what to say.

"Are you mad at me?"

"No."

"You got quiet."

"I'm annoyed but I'm not mad. I wish she would just leave you alone."

"That makes two of us. I wish I could tell her I have a girlfriend. It would make my life easier." He looked at Sydney expectantly.

"Not yet."

He growled and kept his eyes on the road.

"Coen?"

"Baby?"

"I appreciate you being honest with me about Audrey but please keep it to yourself from now on."

"What?"

"I just don't want to hear about her. It bothers me."

"Are you sure?"

"I trust you. All it does is make me jealous and angry. I would rather not know about it if it just makes me upset."

He nodded. "Okay. I won't say anything anymore."

"Thank you."

He wrapped his arm around her shoulder. "You're really amazing, Sydney. Any other girl with your abilities would hunt her down and knock her out."

"Well, you did love her at one point. How can I do that to someone you used to care about?"

He laughed. "She's a fucking bitch and I hate her. Don't ever hold back a punch on my account. I couldn't care less about her. Once she insulted you, I lost all respect for her. In fact, I would enjoy seeing you beat her senseless."

She smiled. "I still couldn't do that. That isn't why I started training."

He kept his mouth closed. Sydney knew he wanted to ask why she started training but he held it back.

He pulled into the parking lot then climbed out. Sydney followed behind him. After they got their ice cream, they headed down to the beach and started walking.

"What did you do while I was at work?"

"I thought about you."

"Were you touching yourself at the time?"

"No," she said as she blushed. "You still haven't shown me how."

"That's right. How could I forget?"

"I have no idea." She picked at her ice cream while he devoured his. After he threw his cup in a trash can, he wrapped his arm around her shoulder and held her close. The sun was setting over the horizon, making the sky splash with blue, gold, and orange. The seagulls flew overhead, looking for any leftover food in the sand. Palm trees lined the beach and provided long shadows of shade. When the waves crashed against the shore, it stilled both of their hearts.

"It means the world to me that you trust me," he blurted.

She looked at him. "You're very trustworthy."

160

"Well, I know you didn't always feel that way. I'm glad you changed your mind."

"I was wrong about you. I had it completely wrong, Coen."

"Not really. I'm not the nicest guy. I'm only nice to people I care about. The rest of the time, I'm short and sarcastic."

"So you are a heartbreaker?"

"To a few—not to you."

"That's gives me some hope."

"I'm wrapped around your finger, Syd. Don't ever worry about that."

"I won't." She tossed her ice cream in the garbage.

He grabbed her hand and squeezed it gently. "You've been the most amazing person I've ever met. You make my heart beat like never before. I can't explain it. I—"

"Hide!" She pushed him toward the tree then dragged him behind the stump.

"What the hell?" he whispered.

"Henry and Nancy are walking by," she said as she looked past the tree.

He followed her gaze and watched them. Henry was kicking the sand below his feet and Nancy had her arms crossed over her chest. "So?"

"Well, I don't want them to see us."

He gripped his hair in anger. He thought he was okay with this secret relationship but he wasn't. It pissed him off. Being someone's secret made him feel unwanted and ashamed.

When her friends returned to the sidewalk and disappeared, Sydney breathed a sigh of relief. "They're gone."

"So I can come out now?" he snapped. "I can actually hold your hand and act like your boyfriend because your friends are gone?"

She looked at him and placed her hands on his chest. "Coen, I—"

"Let's go," he said as he pulled away. He returned to the sand and walked back to the sidewalk with her following behind. They were both silent as they walked to the car. When they got inside, Sydney sat by the passenger door, not in the girlfriend seat.

Coen started the engine without speaking. She knew he didn't want her near him.

As they drove home, her heart accelerated with throbbing pain. She felt horrible for hurting Coen. His anger was justified even though he agreed to keep their relationship a secret. Sydney wanted to be open about their relationship but she couldn't do that to Henry. That would have been a horrible way for him to find out. Seeing her holding Coen's hand while they walked on the beach at sunset. It definitely would have made him feel worse.

When they arrived at her house, Coen jumped out of the car and slammed the door behind him. She followed him to the front door.

"Have a good night," he said as he turned away.

"Please don't go."

"I'm pissed right now, Sydney. I really don't want to talk to you."

"Stay," she begged.

His feet were rooted to the ground, unable to move. He was too weak to resist her beautiful voice.

Sydney approached him then wrapped her arms around his neck, pressing her face close to his. He automatically circled her waist with his hands.

"I'm sorry," she whispered. "But what was I supposed to do? Just let him find out like that?"

He breathed through his anger. "You could have dropped my hand and let him see us hanging out together."

"But then he might suspect something."

162

"Good. He'll realize that you are interested in other guys. It will help him move on. Pushing me in the trees is just unacceptable. I don't deserve to be treated like that."

"I know you don't," she whispered. "But I told you I needed more time. Please give me that." She looked him in the eye. "You told me this was fine in the beginning. I love Henry like my own family. I know you were hurt, but please help me through this. I won't hurt him. I refuse to do it. You're just going to have to deal with it." He said nothing, avoiding her gaze. "I hate this as much as you do. I want to climb on top of you and kiss you in front of Audrey. I want to sit next to you in class, and I want to hold your hand when we walk across campus."

"If he sees us again, you can't hide me. I won't touch you or kiss you, but you can't hide me."

She sighed. "Okay."

"And I want to be involved with your friends. When you guys go out, I'm invited."

"Why?"

"I want them to get used to me. I'm your friend, not just your boyfriend. That sounds like a fair compromise."

She was quiet for a moment. "Okay."

"Thank you."

"Are you still mad?"

"Not as much as I was before. Are you mad at me?"

"No. I understand why you're upset even though you told me you would put up with this for a short amount of time."

"That's the key word; short."

She pulled her hands away. "You can go if you want."

"Do you want me to?"

"Not at all."

He sighed. "So, we're okay?"

"I think we settled this issue—for now."

"I'm sorry I got upset. I just hated being pushed in the trees like that. It's like you're embarrassed of me."

"That couldn't be further from the truth and you know it."

"Sorry. I just got caught up with my emotions."

"I'm sorry too. You deserve more than this, Coen. I admit that."

"Well, I'll wait for you."

"Thank you."

"But I meant what I said. I won't put up with this for long."

"I know." She opened the door then walked inside.

He followed behind and they sat on the couch, saying nothing for a while.

"So, what do you want to do?" he asked.

"I like doing this."

"Can I sleep here tonight?"

She smiled. "I was hoping you would."

"I like sleeping with you, even though we don't get much sleep," he said with a smile.

"Me too."

They left the couch and walked into her bedroom.

When he shut the door, he looked at her. "It's your turn tonight."

"What do you mean?"

"You get to lose control and I'll make sure nothing happens."

"So we trade off?"

"I think that's fair." He took off his shirt and she marveled at the sight. He stared into her eyes as she watched him. When she licked her lips, his spine shivered. He took off his jeans then stood in his boxers. She was frozen as he came over to her and stripped her clothes away. When her shirt came off, she shivered so he pulled her close to him. He kneeled down and removed her shorts.

"I could stare at this all day," he said as he kissed her stomach. He stood up then guided her to the bed. He climbed on top of her then rubbed his nose against hers. "Are you ready to learn?"

Her heart accelerated in her chest. She was excited but also ashamed.

"Don't be embarrassed," he said. "This is hot."

"Really?"

"Hell yes it is." He pulled down her underwear then tossed it on the floor.

"You'll stay in control?"

"I promise," he said as he looked her in the eye.

"Okay."

"Now let me get you ready." He leaned in and kissed her gently, making her melt. She gripped his back and slid her hands across his body. When she reached her hand to his crotch, she wasn't thinking. He let her touch his erection for a second before he pulled her hand away. "We're doing you right now." He reached his hand down and touched her clitoris gently. She moaned for him. "I think you're ready." He inserted two fingers inside her then pulsed gently.

She cupped his face and pulled him closer to her.

"Do you feel that?"

"Oh—yeah."

"Now I'm going to bend my fingers and touch your G spot." When he rubbed her, she knew he hit his mark. She moaned loudly. "I found it," he said with a smile. "You can feel the different texture when you touch it. That's how you'll know."

"Okay," she whispered.

He moved his thumb to her clitoris and started to rub it in circles.

Her body ignited in pleasure as she felt him touch her with such precision. She was losing control and it felt amazing. He increased the pressure as she gripped him harder.

"I want you," she whispered.

"This is me, baby," he said as he looked into her eyes. He pulled his hand out. "It's your turn."

She kissed him. "I like it when you do it."

"Come on. It'll feel good."

"I feel dirty."

"You should. I like it when you're dirty." He grabbed her hand and brought it to her entrance. He guided her fingers inside her.

She gasped as she fingered herself.

Coen pulled off his boxers and started to rub himself. With a shaky breath, he said, "Find the spot I told you about."

"Oh," she said when she found it.

He pulled his hand from himself then pressed her thumb over her clitoris. "Like this," he said as he rubbed it.

She moaned.

"You feel that?"

"Yeah."

"Okay." He grabbed himself again and leaned over her, looking in her eyes as he jerked himself. He pressed his lips against hers while they touched themselves. Sydney still felt connected to him even though they were responsible for their own pleasure.

"Baby, I want you to picture me when you finger yourself."

"Yeah."

"Tell me when you're about to come."

She moaned. "I feel it."

"Keep going." He rubbed himself harder. "I'm there, Sydney," he said with a heavy breath. "I just need you to meet me."

She rubbed her clitoris harder. She felt the formation of the orgasm start and spread through her body.

166

It tingled her fingers and her toes. Her lower stomach throbbed with release. "Coen, I'm there."

He looked into her eyes. "Let go, baby. Come on."

She felt herself crumble under her own ministrations. She fingered herself faster as she convulsed under her own movements. "Oh—god."

Coen bit her lip as he came onto her skin. "Yeah."

When she finished, she pulled her fingers out and rested them on her stomach. "Wow."

"You wish you had learned that sooner, huh?"

"Yeah. But I still like it better when you do it."

"Well, I'm not always here."

"I want you to be."

He rubbed his nose against hers. "I hope that happens someday."

Her eyes softened. "Me too."

He kissed her. "Do you still feel dirty?"

"Filthy."

He smiled. "There's nothing wrong with satisfying yourself. But after we have sex, I doubt you will anymore. I'll please you all the time."

She whimpered. "I want to have sex now."

"I do too."

"Then why don't we?"

He was quiet for a long time. "We aren't ready."

"But I really care about you, Coen. I want to be with you all the time."

He stared into her eyes. "I'll make love to you after Henry knows the truth."

"Why then?"

"Then I'll know that you're really serious about me."

"I am serious."

"And I'll know something else as well."

"What?"

"You'll have to wait and see."

## 14

After Sydney finished cleaning all the tanks, she walked through the lobby toward the break room so she could take her fifteen minute break. When she saw Dr. Goldstein enter through the front doors, her heart raced. Maybe she could talk to him and bring up his research project. But then the depression descended. The guy couldn't even remember her name. She knew it was pointless. Instead of acknowledging him, she turned toward the break room.

"Sydney?"

She stopped and turned around. She was speechless for a moment, shocked that he addressed her by her correct name, not Stacy. "Yes?"

He smiled as he approached her. "I heard that you are quite the student."

Her heart moved into her throat. She wasn't sure if she was dreaming or if this was really happening. Was he talking to her? He knew she was a good student? "Thanks."

"I'm conducting research on great white sharks next week. My team and I are going out to the open ocean for a few days to study their ability to dilute and concentrate salt based on their location in the ocean. Perhaps if we understand this physiological process, we can adapt it to humans."

She already knew everything about his research. He didn't need to tell her any of that. Her mouth dropped open like she was meeting a rockstar. She closed her mouth then cleared her throat. "That sounds fascinating."

"Thank you. I need an undergraduate student to help with the data collecting. Would you be interested?"

She jumped on her toes. "Are you serious?"

He smiled. "Yes. I heard you would be worthy of my time."

"Yes! I would love to. I'm so honored that you even asked me."

He nodded. "That's wonderful. I look forward to working with you."

"Thank you so much," she said as she clapped her hands.

He walked away. "Talk to you soon."

"Bye!" she said as she hopped on her toes. She turned into the break room then pulled her phone from her pocket.

"Hey, baby," Coen said.

Her words came out in a rush. "Oh my god, Dr. Goldstein just invited me on his research trip into the ocean to study great white sharks and he said I could collect data for him and spend a few days with them on the boat!" She took a deep breath before she screamed into the phone. "He actually asked me to go with him. I can't believe this! This is so awesome."

"That's great. I'm happy for you."

"I'm so excited. When he asked me, I almost peed myself."

"I'm glad you're never that excited to see me."

"I'm too happy to care about your insults."

"When do you get off?"

"Soon."

"Can I see you for a little while?"

"Do you wanna come to the aquarium? You can meet Rose."

"Your dolphin friend?"

"Yeah."

"That sounds like fun."

"I can get you in through the back. No one is here right now because we're closed. Just me and Dr. Goldstein."

"I'll be right over."

"Okay." She hung up and waited for him to text her when he arrived. When he did, she went to the back of the facility and opened the door for him. He slipped inside without anyone noticing.

She wrapped her arms around his waist and kissed him. "Hey."

He rubbed his nose against hers. "Hello, gorgeous."

She took his hand and pulled him away. "Come on."

"Do you think she'll like me?"

"Of course. Rose loves everyone."

They walked to the outside pool then kneeled at the edge. The dolphins were swimming near the bottom of the pool, next to the glass viewing window.

"How do you get her attention?" he asked.

"Like this." She tapped the water ten times then pulled her hand away. A moment later, Rose came to the surface with a loud squeal. She moved her head toward the wall and let Sydney pet her. "Isn't she beautiful?"

Coen said nothing as he stared at Sydney, a smile on his face. She gently caressed the rubber flesh of the dolphin's skin then kissed Rose on the nose.

"I'm getting a little jealous," he whispered.

She kissed the dolphin again. "I love you."

The dolphin squealed.

"Can I touch her?" he asked.

"Yes." She looked at Rose. "This is my boyfriend, Coen. He's very special."

The dolphin looked at him then moved closer.

Coen chuckled as he ran his hands over the wet skin. "It's very nice to meet you."

Sydney reached over and touched the side of her head. "Whenever I want to talk to someone, I come to her. She always seems to understand what I'm saying." Coen watched her while she spoke, still rubbing the dolphin. "Animals are better than humans. They aren't complicated

171

or evil. They do what they have to do to survive. And they have emotions just as strong as we do. Whenever I cry, she knows."

"You cry in front of her?"

"Sometimes," she said quietly. "She makes me feel better."

He smiled at the dolphin, who was rubbing her head against his hand. "It's hard not to love her. She reminds me of Brutus."

"I wish I could take her home with me."

"You would," he said with a laugh.

She stared at the dolphin affectionately while Coen stared at Sydney's face, mesmerized by her beautiful features. He wished she would confide her secrets to him but he decided not to pester her about it. She obviously wasn't comfortable yet. She grabbed a fish from a bucket then fed it to Rose, who took it under the surface as she ate it.

Coen stood up. "Are you ready to go?"

"Yeah." She smoothed the wrinkles of her jumpsuit. "Sorry that I don't look my best."

"You always look your best."

"Whatever."

"I'm not a liar, Syd."

She avoided his gaze. They returned to the main building and she clocked out and changed. They left the building and locked the door behind them. After Coen walked her to the car, he turned to her.

"I guess I'll see you tomorrow."

She frowned. "Could you sleep with me tonight?"

"Well, I've fallen behind on my studies. I really need to hit the books."

She hid the disappointment with a smile. The idea of sleeping alone was torturous. Coen was the first person she had reached out to, and now she felt stupid for doing it. But she understood that he had other responsibilities. She had been monopolizing his time for the past few weeks. "Okay."

He looked at her. "It's not that I don't want to."

"I know," she said with another fake smile. "I'll see you tomorrow."

He kissed her on the forehead. "I know you'll be in my dreams tonight."

"Will they be dirty dreams?"

He smiled. "They'll be filthy."

"Good." She turned around and got inside her Jeep. She wanted to hide the despair on her face before he got a glimpse. She pulled out of the parking lot and headed home. She thought about calling him and asking him to study in her bed while she slept but she refused to do that. It was too needy and pathetic. Never in her life had she been as clingy as she was with Coen. Whenever he wasn't there, she wished he was. She could call Henry but she didn't feel comfortable lying beside him. It could only be Coen. He was the one.

After she got inside her house, she went into her bedroom and started to read a book, hoping it would take her mind off her pain. School and work had minimized her thoughts but they came roaring back at the first opportunity.

When her eyes finally started to droop, she let herself fall asleep. Her slumber was dreamless and wonderful. Perhaps the nightmares had stopped because Coen made her feel safe. Just when she was in a deep part of her sleep cycle, it happened.

Sydney couldn't see herself, but she knew she was just sixteen. Her breasts weren't full like they were now and her hips weren't as wide. She was thin and weak, frail like a plastic doll.

She was sitting in her car by the railroad tracks, watching the train speed by every hour. Mom and Dad had gotten into another fight. She wasn't sure what they were arguing about. It seemed like they always fought. When her cell phone rang, she answered it.

"What?" she snapped.

"Where are you?" her father asked calmly.

"Leave me alone."

"I asked you a question, Syd."

She said nothing.

"Your mother and I fight like other adults. It's normal."

"Why is she so mean to you? Why does she hit you?"

He sighed. "She can't control her emotions like I can."

"Because she's drunk," she snapped. "Why did you even marry her?"

"I love her, that's why."

"Well, you shouldn't."

"It seems like you can't control your emotions either."

She said nothing.

"Are you by the railroad tracks?"

"I'm not coming home," she snapped.

"That's fine. I'll come get you."

"No."

"See you soon." He hung up.

Her father hardly ever lost his temper or got mad. He somehow always calmed her down even when she didn't want to feel calm. His abilities were supernatural at times. Sydney hugged her jacket tighter around her and searched for headlights in the distance, knowing her father would be there soon. The faint sound of the train horn sounded in the distance. She continued to look for the station wagon he drove, the hideous car that he refused to get rid of.

If Sydney had to choose which parent she liked more, it would be her father in a heartbeat. Her mom was catty and mean, superficial and blatantly stupid. Her only good quality was her features. That's it. She suspected her father must have fallen under her spell and ignored all of her shortcomings. Sydney was thankful that she received the perfect genetics from both of them; her mother's looks and her father's brains. She did have some physical similarities to her father. They both had the same brown hair and startling green eyes.

The fog was heavy but she could distinguish an approaching car driving down the road. The train was speeding by on its way through the city. Sydney knew she had a few extra minutes to herself because the crossing rails would fall down in just a second, trapping her father on the other side of the road. Her father's car continued to drive, not slowing down. The bars never fell.

She sat up in her seat and honked the horn as loud as she could. "Stop!"

The train honked its horn but it was too late. It collided with the station wagon just as it passed through the gate, crushing and sending it into the air.

Sydney tried to wake up but she couldn't. She hated reliving this dream over and over. It was more painful every time. She screamed but her own voice fell on deaf ears. She was trapped in her own nightmares.

Suddenly, her stepfather chased her through the house with a bat. He always beat her for random reasons. Sometimes, he was just drunk and wanted to hit her. Other times, she said the wrong thing. His son would sit by and watch as she ran into the closet and held the door closed, hoping he would stop waiting for her and just collapse in a drunken stupor or fall asleep. Her mother never even attempted to help her. She turned a blind eye.

When her stepfather slammed the bat into the door, pushing the wood in, she screamed. The sound of her voice finally startled her from sleep. She sat up and gripped the blanket, sweat drenched on her skin. Crying hysterically, she reached for her phone and called Coen without thinking.

"You miss me?" he asked with a smile in his voice.

She kept crying, holding herself tightly. "It's all my fault. I—I deserve this."

His tone immediately changed. "Are you okay?"

"No."

"Are you hurt?"

She spoke, but her words were incoherent through her sobbing. She rocked herself back and forth, trying to get rid of the vision in her mind. Her father's crash was etched on the back of her eyelids. She still felt like her stepfather was trying to catch her.

"I'm coming. Stay on the phone with me."

She nodded even though he couldn't see her. She cried, trying to stifle her tears with her palm.

Coen slammed the car door shut and started the engine. "I'm almost there," he said quietly.

She said nothing.

"You're going to be okay."

She sniffed.

When he pulled up outside, he left the car and ran to the door. She hung up without saying goodbye then walked to the entryway. When she unlocked the door, he burst in and wrapped his arms around her.

Sydney immediately felt better once she could collapse against him. He held her tightly to his chest, running his fingers through her hair. She continued to cry, unable to stop. Coen grabbed her keys from the counter then guided her outside.

She was too upset to ask where they were going. She remembered walking to the crashed car, seeing her father's eyes wide open. He was dead before the ambulance could get there. If she hadn't been a brat, it never would have happened. Her father died because of her stupidity.

Coen helped her inside the car and put on her safety belt. She stared straight ahead without thinking about anything but the loss of her father. He turned on the engine then left the driveway, driving down the deserted streets of the city. Her cries trickled down but a few tears still fell. His arm was secured around her shoulders, reminding her that she was safe.

When they pulled up to the aquarium, she finally found her voice. "What are we doing here?"

He grabbed the keys then picked her up in his arms, carrying her to the back entrance. When he reached the door, he picked up the right key and got it open. Sydney didn't understand what they were doing there, but she followed his lead.

When they walked inside, he grabbed her hand and led her to the outside pool. The door was unlocked so they just walked in.

Sydney stopped when she saw the dolphin pool. "Why did you bring me here?"

Coen kneeled at the edge and tapped the water ten times. "So you could talk to Rose."

Her heart squeezed again but not from pain. It was the sweetest thing anyone had ever done for her.

He held his hand out to her. "Come on."

She walked to him and sat at the edge of the pool. Rose popped up a moment later, squealing happily. Sydney rubbed her head while the tears fell down her face. Rose became quiet when she realized her friend was sad. She rubbed her head against Sydney's hand.

Coen sat beside her and said nothing.

The waves could be heard crashing against the shore down below. The lights from the pool flickered across the wall, lighting their faces and the water in the pool.

"I had a dream," she said quietly. She lowered her legs into the pool and the dolphin rested its head on her thighs. Rose looked up at Sydney, her mouth slightly opened. "My dad—he died." Coen didn't move but he was hanging on every word she said. "I saw the crash again. It was my fault he was there. If I wasn't throwing a tantrum, he wouldn't have been there at all. The train wouldn't have hit him."

Coen moved closer to her, pressing his shoulder against hers.

"My parents were fighting and I took off, sneaking out. When my dad found out I was gone, he came after me. When he crossed the railroad tracks, the crossing bars didn't drop. He was in such a hurry to get to me that he didn't even notice the train." She took a deep breath and the tears started to fall again.

Coen wrapped his arm around her shoulder. "Baby, it's not your fault."

"Yes, it is!"

He fell silent.

"It's completely my fault. He's dead because of me. Dead."

He rubbed his hand down her back. "Is today the anniversary of his passing?"

She was quiet for a moment. "Yes."

"I'm sorry I didn't stay with you like you asked. I would have if you had told me that."

"I don't want to be needy."

He grabbed her face and directed her gaze on him. "You aren't needy. And even if you are, I love it when you need me. You can ask me for anything and I will do everything in my power to make it happen. I love it when you lean on me, ask me to hold you, confide in me. I want you to be needy. I know you've never been that way in your whole life, choosing to stand on your own two feet and work out your own problems, but everything is different now. We split the load—always."

"Really?"

178

"Yes. Don't be afraid to ask me for things. I will always be there for you. If I had known what today was, I would have been there for you. All you have to do is ask."

"Okay."

He kissed her forehead. "I would like to be what Rose is to you. Your best friend."

Henry was always her best friend but she realized that was changing—it should change. "You are my best friend."

"Good. Thank you for telling me about your dad. I know that was difficult for you."

She nodded.

"My mom cheated on my dad when I was in high school. They were legally separated for two years before they got back together. It was a difficult time for me and my brother. We stayed with my dad while she lived alone. We weren't even allowed to see her."

She stared at him, speechless. "I—I'm sorry."

"They got back together so it's okay. But it will never be the same. That trust is gone."

"Thank you for telling me that."

"And I used to have a sister."

The depression in his voice frightened her. He sounded upset before, but his voice had fallen to a lower level. "You had a sister?"

He nodded. "She died."

"How?"

"She was a lot older than me. When I was in high school, she was already in college. She had a boyfriend that my parents liked. When my sister and her boyfriend took me out to ice cream, they got into a fight. He had a horrible temper and he started hitting her, beating her. I did everything I could protect her, got a few broken ribs and a skull fracture, but in the end I couldn't save her. I was too small and had no idea how to fight."

She had no idea what to say. That sudden revelation was too horrible to even imagine.

"That's why I started learning martial arts. No one will ever touch the people I love, not while I'm living."

"I'm sorry," she said as she grabbed his hand.

He nodded and blinked his eyes. If he had tears, he fought them. "I've become a different person since it happened. I'm mean, harsh, and sarcastic all the time. It took me a long time to deal with it, to move on from what happened. During that time, I did a lot of things I regret, was darker than I meant to be. That's where my reputation stems from even though no one knows what happened."

"What happened to the boyfriend?"

"He's in jail for life."

She nodded, not knowing what else to say.

"I've never told anyone before. You're the first."

"I feel honored."

"And I'm honored that you told me something so private about you."

"Well, you are my best friend."

He stared at her for a long time without saying anything. She knew he was waiting for her to reveal her other secret, the one he was desperate to know, but she wasn't ready for that. He sighed when he realized she wasn't going to confide in him. "I know you are going to be angry for me asking this, but I have to." He paused. "Does Henry know about your dad?"

"No," she said quickly.

His eyes widened. "So, I'm the first person you told?"

She nodded.

"That means a lot to me." He grabbed her hand and squeezed it. "It really does."

"You mean so much to me, Coen."

"And you mean everything to me."

Rose slid back in the pool then started flapping her fins together, screeching as she danced. The sight made Sydney laugh. Coen watched the light return to her face. He was always interested in animals but he never connected to them in the way she did. They seemed to communicate with her on a different level.

"Thank you for bringing me here."

"I knew you needed your friend."

"She can be your friend too."

Rose clapped her fins and screeched.

"I would like that," he said with a smile.

Sydney pulled her legs out of the water then stood up. "I'm ready to go home."

"Okay. I'm tired."

"Me too."

"And please let me sleep with you."

"I expected nothing less."

They left the aquarium hand in hand. When they returned to her shack under the trees, they both lay in bed and said nothing. Coen ran his fingers through her hair while she looked into his eyes, taking solace in his presence. She hoped he would chase the nightmares away, holding her tightly in his arms.

Sydney cupped his cheek and pressed her face close to his, listening to him breathe.

"Go to sleep, baby. I'll be your dream catcher."

She closed her eyes then fell sleep. She dreamt of swimming with dolphins in the open sea with Coen swimming alongside her. Her lungs didn't restrict with pain and there were no tears in her eyes. The tension around her heart and shoulders was absent as Coen caressed her skin softly. There was no pain or fear. She was safe and nothing could hurt her, not when Coen was watching over her.

# 15

"How was your night?" Sydney asked as she drank her coffee.

"It was okay," Henry said quietly. "I studied."

Their relationship was still awkward. Sydney tried not to think about it but the tension was still in the air. She wanted to go back to how they were but she knew they couldn't. Everything was different now.

"What did you do?" he asked, looking out the window. He hardly ever looked at her anymore.

"I...I just stayed home."

"When I went to work, it said you used your key to get inside at three in the morning. What were you doing there?"

"Oh—I left my books in my locker."

"Why did you need them?"

"My wallet was in the bag."

"Oh. I could have gotten them for you in the morning."

"Well, it's already done now."

He nodded.

Lillian, a girl from Sydney's English class, walked by their booth. "Good morning," she said with a smile.

"Hey." Sydney waved. "We just need some grub before we go to school."

She patted her stomach. "Me too. Are you going to Liz's party tonight?"

"Yeah. Are you?"

"I'll be there." She looked at Henry. "Hello."

"Hey," he said with a nod.

"Well, I'll see you guys later." She walked away and sat down in a booth across the restaurant. Lillian was tall and thin with blonde hair that reached her shoulders.

She was very pretty. Guys were usually tailing her everywhere she went.

"She's cute," Sydney said as she ate her waffle.

Henry looked out the window and said nothing.

"I don't think she's seeing anyone."

He still said nothing.

"Maybe you should talk to her. I know she thinks you're cute."

"I'm in love with you," he blurted, finally looking at her. She flinched as his heated gaze landed on her. "And you're just making this worse. I know how to pick up chicks and I know how to get laid. I'll do it when I'm ready."

"I'm sorry," she said quietly.

He pushed his plate away, no longer hungry.

She sighed. "We are never going to be back to what we were, huh?"

"We will," he said as he looked at her. "I...I just need some time."

"Okay."

"Have you ever wanted something so bad you would kill for it? You would do anything at all to make it happen? That's how I feel about you. I know you said you don't feel the same way, but I can't change these feelings instantly. They are there and will be there for a while. I don't know what to do."

"Maybe we should stop seeing each other."

He shook his head. "You're my best friend. I can't do that."

"Just for a short time."

"No."

"Start dating."

"That wouldn't be fair to them. I'd be using them to get over you, the girl of my dreams."

She looked at her coffee, avoiding his gaze. The intensity of his emotions startled her. She knew he had feelings for her but she didn't realize how much he loved her. "You haven't been with anyone in two years?"

"No," he said quietly. "I fucked a few girls because I was horny. I thought about you the entire time."

His vulgarity was shocking. He had never spoken to her like that before. She never suspected he would sleep around.

"I haven't been with anyone for a year. After a while, it got too hard. I felt like I was cheating on you or something."

She said nothing, unsure what to say.

"I would do anything just to have one chance with you." He looked at her hopefully. "We have nothing to lose. Our relationship is already totally screwed up and you understand the depth of my feelings. We may as well give it a shot. You aren't seeing anyone and neither am I. We don't even have to tell anyone."

"I already said no, Henry."

He rested his elbows on the table. "Why?"

"I'm just not attracted to you in that way."

"Let me kiss you and see what happens."

"Henry, the last thing I want to do is hurt you, but you keep making me do it. This is making me uncomfortable and I want you to stop asking me. Please."

He stared at her for a moment then reached across the table, touching her hand. "I'm sorry. I didn't mean to scare you."

"It's okay."

"I'll stop. I don't want to chase you away. I would rather have some of you than none of you."

"What if we can't work this out?"

"There's nothing to work out. You don't love me and I love you. That's the end of the story."

"But what if you never move on?"

"I will eventually. Don't worry about that."

She nodded her head. "I just don't want our relationship to change."

"It won't. I'll move on and find someone else so when you—do get a boyfriend—I won't be—totally miserable."

He could barely finish his sentence because he was so distraught over the idea of her seeing someone else. How could she ever tell him about Coen? It would kill him. He said their relationship would never change but it would. He would disappear and never speak to her again.

"Hey," he said as he looked at her. "Don't be sad."

"Maybe we should stop talking, Henry. I feel like I'm being selfish."

"How?"

"How are you supposed to get over me if we're still best friends? You see me every day. It's never going to work."

"No. It'll be fine. I don't want to risk this friendship. I value it. Please don't think like that. If you stopped talking to me, it would only hurt more."

"Are you sure?"

"Yes," he said with smile. It was weak but he tried anyway. He leaned back in his chair. "Let's talk about something else."

"Okay."

"What's up with Coen?"

Her heart fell. "What do you mean?"

"I think he's into you."

"What? Why?"

"He's always around now. He came out of nowhere. And he always stares at you. He tries to be discreet about it but I've noticed it."

"He's just a friend. After I started tutoring him, we just got closer."

Henry's eyes widened. "What do you mean by that?"

"I just mean I don't think he's an asshole anymore."

He nodded. "Okay. So you aren't into him?"

She was backed into a corner. She hated lying to Henry. She loved him and didn't want to hurt him, but on the other hand, she was hurting Coen, her boyfriend. This would be so much easier if she never found out about Henry's feelings.

Henry leaned back in his chair, worry plagued on his face. "Sydney?"

"No," she said quickly. "I'm not."

He breathed a sigh of relief. He tried to hide his obvious happiness but he was failing miserably. Sydney knew she couldn't tell him the truth. It would cripple him. She would have to wait until he started dating before she even considered it. She knew Coen wouldn't be happy about that. But he would wait like he promised.

After they paid the tab, they left for campus in their separate cars. Coen was already sitting in his car in the parking lot, waiting for her. He tried to act inconspicuous when he approached them.

"Hey. Thank god it's Friday," he said.

"I know," she said with a smile. She couldn't stop her lips from stretching across her face. Coen made her so happy. She wanted to kiss him, press his body next to hers, but she had to bottle all those feelings inside. It was becoming harder by the day. When she looked into his eyes, she saw the same expression.

Henry nodded but said nothing.

The three of them walked to their first class and took their seats. The lecture dragged on forever. Sydney tried to concentrate but she kept fantasizing about Coen making love to her. They had been together for a few weeks and she was ready to move their relationship to the next level. It was hard to see him naked and not want him. He must've felt the same way. He said they would wait until she told Henry but she didn't know if she could wait that long. After she told him about her father, she knew he was the right person for her. That was a secret she had kept to herself for years. The feelings she had for Coen were powerful and unbreakable. She wanted to feel him inside of her.

She finished the rest of her classes with Henry right beside her. He was quiet for most of the day, avoiding her look and not being talkative. Since she knew he was in so much pain, she respected his silence. A part of her was angry that Henry was so in love with her because it halted her relationship with Coen, but she also felt angry toward herself. She must have led him on without realizing it.

When she finally walked into the library to tutor Coen, she was so relieved. She wanted to be with him, kiss his lips and feel his skin. Acting indifferent to him all day was pure torture. When she walked inside, he looked up at her.

"Can we go to my place?" she asked.

"What's wrong with the library?"

"If we're going to study, why don't we do it at my place?" She sat on his lap and immediately felt his boner spring to life. "And we aren't even going to be studying so what's the point of staying here?"

"At least we know we won't get out of control here."

"I want to get out of control."

He stared at her for a moment. "Did you tell Henry?"

She sighed. "No."

"Then my answer is no."

"I want to go home anyway."

"Why?"

"I want to fool around."

"That sounds tempting."

"Let's get it out of our system before the party."

"Why? Because you're going to ignore me the entire time?" The anger in his voice was palpable. She knew his patience about their secret relationship was waning.

"Do you want to come or not?"

"I can jerk off at home."

"Why are you being an ass right now?"

He sighed. "You're right. I'm sorry. I'm just sick of lying to everyone."

"I know," she said as she cupped his cheeks. "Just a little while longer."

"Promise?"

"I promise."

"Okay. Let's go."

They left the library and walked to the parking lot. After an innocent kiss, they drove back to her shack near the beach. As soon as they left their cars and walked inside, Sydney felt the arousal course through her. Ever since she opened up to him, she felt a stronger connection to Coen. She wanted to be with him, share her soul with his. It was so powerful she felt herself shake. She wanted Coen not just for now, but forever.

She wrapped his arms around his neck and pressed her forehead against his. "Make love to me, Coen."

He kissed her neck then her lips, igniting her in a blast of heat. "I would love to, baby." He guided her down the hall then entered the bedroom, shutting the door behind him. He grabbed her shirt then pulled it from her body.

Sydney felt her heart accelerate as she realized they were really doing this. She wanted him so bad she thought she would scream. It felt right with him, different than with Aaron. As far as she was concerned, Aaron never happened. It was only Coen. It had always been him. Her desire for him wasn't just for lust. She wanted to feel him inside her, commit to him in a deeper way. Her heart hammered in her chest for him. There was no one else in the world she wanted more. She grabbed his shirt and pulled it off, admiring the muscles of his chest. With steady hands, she unbuttoned his jeans and pulled them down, taking his underwear with them. When she saw his cock, she moaned. It was bigger than any other she had seen. She knew it was going to be a tight fit, but she looked forward to trying to take him.

Coen unclasped her bra then removed her jeans and underwear. He stood in front of her then pressed himself against her, placing his erection against her stomach.

She dug her fingers into his hair and kissed him as she lay down on the bed. When he followed her, she wrapped her legs around his waist. Her hands ran wild over his body, feeling every inch of his skin. He was the most beautiful thing she had ever seen. His soul was even more beautiful. When she looked into his blue eyes, she saw everything she cherished.

He ran his fingers though her hair as he pressed his lips against hers. The touch was gentle and loving then it ignited in deep passion. She grabbed his shoulders and tilted her hips closer to him, wanting him to enter her. Her pussy was so wet she didn't need any further stimulation. She was never more sure of anything in her life than she was of Coen.

He pressed his tip against her entrance but didn't move inside.

She scratched her nails down his back, eager to feel him within her.

He continued to kiss her but didn't make the final plunge. The wait was killing her. She thought she would come just from feeling his head.

"Coen," she said into his mouth. She pulled his hips toward her but he didn't move. "I want you inside me."

"You do?"

"God, yes. I've wanted you forever. You mean everything to me."

"I do?"

"Of course."

He stopped kissing her then grabbed her phone from the nightstand. His voice came out serious. "Then tell him the truth."

She leaned back and looked at him. He was holding the phone in her face. "What?"

"The sooner you tell him, the sooner I'll make love to you. Now make the call."

"I told you he isn't ready yet."

"Then I'm not ready."

"You're being unfair."

"I told you we wouldn't have sex until he knew the truth. So, now you need to uphold your end of the deal."

"I will tell him. I promise."

"That's not enough."

"I can't wait any longer. Coen, I want you. I—I—"

"What?" he asked. "You what?"

"I...I want to be with you. I want to feel that connection with you. The way I feel about you is different than anything I've ever experienced. Please don't make me wait."

"You're the one making us wait. I've been a one-night stand to so many girls. They just fuck me because they know I'll get them off. I want to be with someone who wants to commit to me. You won't even tell anyone about me. How do I know you aren't just going to hurt me?"

"I would never do that. You know how I feel about you."

"Do I? If you really wanted to be with me, you would tell Henry."

"He's my family. Why don't you understand that?"

"It's been weeks, Syd. It's time to tell him. If he's really your friend, he'll still be around."

"I don't want to hurt him."

"Well, you're hurting me. I hate for it to come to his, but it's him or me, Syd. You keep your boyfriend or you keep your friend."

"Please don't do this to me."

"I've been very patient, but I'm not doing it anymore. He's always going to be in pain over you. I'm not gonna wait forever. If you respect me, you'll do this for me."

"He's everything to me."

"And what am I? I thought I was."

"Of course you are."

"I'm not asking you to stop being best friends with him. I'm just asking you to publicly recognize me as your boyfriend. I can't sleep with you without that guarantee. I don't want to get hurt again."

"I'll never hurt you. You can trust me."

"You are hurting me now."

"Coen—"

"Sydney, I admire your loyalty to those you love, but this is bullshit. His feelings aren't your problem and you shouldn't suffer for it. I know the guy loves you so he will understand the truth. He wants you to be happy, even if it isn't with him."

She said nothing, staring into his blue eyes. She didn't know what to say. It was either hurt Coen or hurt Henry. She wished the situation was different.

Coen returned his phone to the nightstand. "I'll give you some time to think about it." He got off the bed and dressed himself.

"Please don't go," she begged.

"Give me your answer tonight at the party. That's plenty of time for you to make your final decision."

She got up and wrapped her arms around him. "Coen, stay with me."

"No."

"Please."

"I've been more than patient and more than understanding about the whole thing. It's your turn to make a compromise." He walked to the front door and she trailed behind him. "I'll see you later."

"Coen?"

"What?"

"Please don't do this."

His eyes dimmed, full of pain. "You've already made your decision." He got into his car then drove out of the driveway.

Sydney stood there, paralyzed. Tears spilled from her eyes as she stood on her porch completely naked. She waited for him to come back but he never did. When she called him, he didn't answer. She didn't know where he lived so she couldn't follow him. She had to wait until the party.

She walked back inside and sat on her bed, still crying. Perhaps she should just tell Henry the truth. Even though it would hurt him, he wouldn't want her to be unhappy. If Henry loved her as much as he said he did, he would want her to be with Coen. She knew he would. She wiped her tears away then got dressed, wondering what to say to Henry. How she should tell him the truth. Nothing came to mind.

Henry arrived at the door an hour later. She took a deep breath before she opened it. He was wearing jeans and a plain shirt. His brown hair was slightly shorter than usual.

"Did you get a haircut?" she asked.

"Thanks for noticing," he said with a smile. He stared at her tan legs under her shorts and her tight fitting shirt. "You look lovely."

"Thanks."

"Are you ready to go?"

"Actually, I wanted to talk to you about something."

His smile dropped. "I really don't think I can take anymore, Sydney," he said quietly.

"What?"

"I know you don't want to be with me. I get it. Please stop reminding me."

She sighed. This was going to be even harder than she thought.

"Let me try to move on without talking about it ever again. When you find someone you want to be with, it's going to kill me, and I want to be as over you as possible when that time comes. Imagining you with someone else makes me want to gag. I'm sorry for being so selfish but it does. I just couldn't handle it."

She bowed her head. How could she tell him that she already moved on with someone else? He was barely holding himself together as it was. Could she hurt him like that just so she could have what she wanted? She didn't want to be a selfish person and that sounded innately selfish.

"Are you ready to go?"

She swallowed the lump in her throat and stopped the tears from falling. "Yeah." Now she couldn't have Coen, the man she wanted. She was really going to lose him.

"Are you okay?" he asked.

"I'm fine."

He stared at her for a long moment. "You seem sad."

"Just tired," she lied.

"Okay." He walked out the door and she followed behind him.

When they got inside the car, she stared out the passenger window, wishing she would just have a heart attack and go to the hospital instead. Then she wouldn't have to go to the party and Coen would be so worried about her that he would drop the Henry issue. She twisted her hands in her lap as her heart accelerated. They were approaching the house and she had nowhere to hide. How could she live without Coen?"

When Henry parked the car, she didn't move from her seat. Coen's car was parked a few feet away. He was already here.

"Are you sure you're alright?" he asked.

"Uh, yeah." She opened the door and got out.

The music could be heard from everywhere around the block. People were smoking outside, a couple was making out against a truck, and a few people were drinking on the front lawn. They walked inside and moved through the crowd of people. People were dancing in the middle of the room, wasted. Henry walked to the back of the house then walked through the back door. People were swimming in the pool while someone barbequed. Sydney scanned the area for Coen but didn't see him anywhere.

"Hey," Laura said as she hugged her. "You look great."

"You too," Sydney said without looking at her.

"I'm so glad this party is at night. I hate wearing sunblock. It makes me break out."

"Totally," Sydney said without thinking.

Nancy nudged her in the arm. "You look like someone just died."

Henry looked at Nancy. "I thought the same thing."

"I'm just tired," she said automatically.

"Well, stop being tired," Laura said.

"Okay," Sydney said.

Derek handed Henry a beer. "About time you got here."

"I had to get gas," he answered.

Sydney crossed her arms over her waist and zoned out. Her friends kept talking but she didn't listen to anything they said. Her thoughts were on Coen. What was she supposed to do? Could she hurt her best friend like that? Could she lose Coen? Everything was so perfect and now it was totally destroyed.

She felt an arm brush her shoulder and she looked up, seeing Coen's face close to hers. Everyone in the circle stopped talking as they watched Coen leaned toward Sydney. His lips were very close to hers, but he said nothing. He stared into her eyes, waiting for her to make her decision.

Sydney knew she had to kiss him in front of Henry if she wanted to keep him, or at least embrace him in some way. Coen kept his eyes glued to hers as he waited for her to make up her mind. She felt Henry stare at her and that stopped her movement. He was her family. She couldn't do that to him, at least not yet. She turned her head away and broke their eye contact.

Coen didn't move for a second. When she looked back at him, she saw the coat of tears in his eyes. Red started to form on his skin. This was agony. The sight brought tears to her eyes. Before she could speak, Coen leaned toward her ear. "Goodbye, Sydney." He left and went back in the house, leaving her completely alone. Her friends were gathered around her, looking at her with confused expressions on their faces. People laughed as the cook flipped a burger patty into the air. The pool water reached over the edge, getting their feet wet. But she didn't notice any of that. All she felt was hollow and empty, as if all the lights from the stars had been sucked away, leaving her universe dark and cold.

# 16

She did nothing that weekend, just stayed in bed, staring at the ceiling. She called Coen a few times but his phone was off. He obviously didn't want to speak to her. Since Henry knew her better than anyone, he knew she was distressed about something. Every time he came by the house, she told him to leave because she had the flu. When he returned with soup, she closed the door in his face then tossed the cup in the garbage. Her appetite was gone. She was dehydrated from all the fluid lost from her tears. She didn't bother to drink anymore because she just didn't feel like it.

Even though she had an English exam on Monday, she didn't study. For the first time, she didn't care about school. The one thing that actually mattered to her was now gone. Every time she thought about telling Henry the truth so she could try to get Coen back, she imagined the hurt on Henry's face. He had been in love with her for two years. She couldn't do that to him. To spare him any pain, she would suffer in his stead. She just wished she didn't have to lose something so important to shelter him.

When Monday arrived, she went to class but Coen completely ignored her, just as she suspected. Her friends noticed her quiet attitude, but whenever they asked about it, she said she was still sick. When they ate in the cafeteria, Coen was nowhere in sight. She took her English exam but she was pretty certain she failed it. When she didn't feel stressed about it, she knew she had hit rock bottom.

After her classes were over, she walked to the library, feeling her heart thud in her chest. She wasn't sure what to say to Coen. She wasn't sure what he would say to her. When she walked into the study room, it was empty. She suspected he wouldn't come but she hoped he would. She was sadly mistaken.

An hour later, she walked to her car then left for the gym. She was certain she would see him there. He couldn't ditch a client and he couldn't call in sick to work every day. She changed then walked into the room, but she was disappointed to find a man she had never seen before.

"Where's Coen?" she asked without saying hello, being completely rude.

"His schedule changed so I'll be training you." He smiled as he walked to her and shook her hand. "Don't worry. I'm perfectly qualified to train you."

"I want Coen," she blurted.

His smile faded. "I'm sorry. I'm the best we have."

She put her bag down and they got to work. During the session, she gave everything in her punches and her kicks, trying to hurt her trainer as much as possible. When he was surprised by her ferocity, he increased his movement, hitting her a few times. The blows hurt but she wanted to feel the pain. After hurting Coen like that, she deserved to suffer. Perhaps if she was in enough pain, she could sleep at night. Nightmares plagued her dreams, and not ones about her father and stepfather. But ones about Coen.

When she finished for the day, she went home. She was irritated to see Henry's car in the driveway.

"Hey," he said as he rose from the porch.

"I'm not feeling well," she said automatically.

"Then why did you go to the gym?"

"Just go, Henry," she snapped.

He grabbed her arm. "We tell each other everything. What's wrong, Sydney? You've been weird since Friday."

"I just want to be alone," she said without looking at him. "Please go away."

"You're scaring me."

She said nothing.

"Did I do something?"

"Of course not," she said quietly. "I...I just want to be alone."

He released his hold. "I'm here if you need me."

"I know, Henry."

"I hope you feel better."

"Yeah." She walked in the house then slammed the door behind her. She raided her cabinets until she found some leftover tequila. She drank it straight from the bottle until her mind felt fuzzy. When she felt on the verge of being totally drunk, she crawled in bed and went to sleep. When she didn't wake up until the following morning, she was relieved. The alcohol stopped the nightmares.

At school, she repeated the same cycle. She only saw Coen in zoology and he acted like she didn't exist. Henry sat beside her while Nancy was on the other side, but she felt alone and afraid. When Aaron cheated on her, it broke her heart, but it was nothing compared to this. She knew it was entirely her fault. She chose this path. If she put herself before Henry, then she wouldn't be in pain, but that was something she couldn't do.

When they had lunch, Henry bought her some vegetarian pizza and set it before her. "Please eat something," he whispered.

"I'm not hungry," she said, blinking back tears. Everything hurt all the time.

Nancy looked at her, concern in her eyes. "What's going on with you?"

"I...I'm just stressed out," she said as she hid her face.

Henry moved to the chair beside her and wrapped his arm around her shoulder, holding her to him. "Please tell us."

"No."

"I'm coming over tonight."

"Leave me alone."

"No."

She moved away from him and grabbed her stuff. "Leave me alone," she said as she walked out. Neither of her friends followed her. Tears fell down her cheeks as she walked across the cafeteria. Her heart fell when she saw Coen sitting with his friends, laughing. When his eyes fell on her, he quickly looked away. Her obvious despair meant nothing to him.

She ditched her last class and just went home. Since she hadn't eaten anything for a few days, she forced herself to snack on crackers in her pantry. She was afraid if she didn't eat, she would die. She drank some water then reached for more tequila. When she realized she had to go to work, she put it down then walked out the door.

Work was the highlight of her week. Having something to distract her mind from the reality of her pain was appreciated. She just cleaned the tanks and took care of the animals, feeding them and changing their boxes. She stopped by to see Rose and cried her heart out while the dolphin wailed, saddened by her friend's despair.

When she got home, Henry, Nancy, Derek, and Laura were all waiting for her. Instead of dealing with them, she backed out of the driveway and took off. They jumped in their cars to follow her, but she evaded their pursuit and parked her car in a parking lot near the ocean. She lay down and stared at the stars until some unearthly hour. When she returned, Henry was still outside, sleeping with his back against her front door.

She walked up the stairs then nudged him to the side. He remained asleep as she walked inside and locked the door behind her. She drank herself to sleep and collapsed on her bed. She didn't wake up because she didn't set an alarm, so when she opened her eyes, it was already noon. She turned on her side and went back to sleep.

A loud knocking on the door made her flinch. She pulled the blankets tighter then closed her eyes. She vaguely heard the door open and someone walk inside. If it was a burglar, she didn't care. They could take whatever they wanted. When her bedroom door opened, she heard someone walk inside. She still didn't turn around.

The bed dipped as someone lay beside her.

"Who is it?" she asked quietly.

"Someone who is very scared for you," Henry said.

"Please leave me alone."

"No."

"I don't feel like hanging out."

"That's fine." He lay on his back and looked up at the ceiling. "I brought veggie tacos from that place you like."

Her stomach growled even though she wasn't hungry.

"Come on. Eat with me," he said as he nudged her. "I know you haven't been healthy. You've already lost like five pounds."

"That isn't possible."

"Well, you look thin."

"Please leave, Henry."

He stood up then pulled her out of bed. "I'm not taking no for an answer."

"Fuck you."

His eyes widened. "Sydney, tell me what the hell happened."

"Just go," she said as she started to cry.

He wrapped her in his arms. "I can't leave you like this."

"I don't want you here."

"Too bad."

He kissed her on the forehead then under her eye. He had never kissed her before and she wasn't sure how she felt about it. She was too depressed to care, but at the same time, it reminded her of Coen, which made her feel even worse.

"Come on, Syd." He picked her up then carried her to the kitchen table. The food was already laid out on plates. "Please eat—for me."

She sighed then grabbed a taco and shoved it into her mouth.

He breathed a sigh of relief and started to eat his burrito.

They said nothing as they sat together. Sydney ate her food slowly, chewing every bite until it was completely disintegrated. She hadn't eaten a meal in so long that she forgot how. Henry glanced at her with worried expressions every few seconds, making sure she was eating.

She finished one taco then pushed the other two away. "Thank you."

"You can't eat anymore?"

"Not without throwing up." She left the table and returned to her bedroom. She closed the door behind her and he didn't follow her. When she heard the television, she knew he was still in the house. As long as he wasn't bothering her, she didn't care.

When she fell asleep, the nightmares returned. Coen was with Audrey, having sex with her in Sydney's bed. It broke her heart and made her break down in tears, screaming hysterically.

Henry burst through the door then woke her up. His presence didn't comfort her like Coen's did, but it was enough to pull her from the nightmare. He lay beside her and wrapped her in his arms. She stared at the wall without saying anything, wishing that Coen was there. If he was, the nightmare wouldn't have happened to begin with.

She didn't go to school the next day and neither did Henry. He made her breakfast then forced her to eat it at the table. Even though she was depressed, she appreciated everything Henry did for her that week. She had been a bitch to him and she knew it.

"I'm sorry about how I've been acting."

He washed his hands and came back to her. "You don't need to apologize."

"Why are you so sweet to me? I don't deserve it."

"I love you," he said as he looked her in the eye. "I always will."

She looked away.

He grabbed her hand and pulled her to a stand. "Let's go to the beach."

"I don't feel like swimming."

"That's fine. You need some fresh air." He grabbed a blanket then pulled her out the front door. They walked to the beach and he laid the blanket on the sand. He helped her sit down before he sat next to her.

The waves crashed against the shore and resonated with her beating heart. The sun was disappearing over the horizon, making the sky shine with different colors. A single star could be seen in the sky. The light breeze ran through her strands of hair and pulled them from her face. This was the best she felt all week. She lay down and stared straight up.

"Thanks for bringing me out here."

He lay beside her, holding her hand in his. "I knew it would make you feel better."

"You know me so well."

"Better than anyone," he said as he sat up and looked down at her.

"I know."

He leaned toward her face. "Are you ready to talk about it?"

"No."

"I really wish you would tell me."

"Please drop it."

"Okay." He continued to stare at her, sadness in his eyes. He leaned farther over her. "Even when you cry, you are the most beautiful woman I've ever seen."

"I can't believe you said that after I've been so rude to you."

He shrugged. "It's nice not having to lie anymore. I always wanted to tell you that I love you. It's nice to finally get it off my chest." He looked at her lips then back at her eyes. She knew what he was thinking. "And I've always wanted to do this." He pressed his lips against hers and held them there, not moving. After a second, his lips caressed hers and she reciprocated. She didn't want to reject his attempt at kissing her, breaking his heart even more, so she let him be. Henry was actually a very good kisser. When he slipped his tongue into her mouth, a part of her enjoyed it, but then Coen came into her mind. They weren't together anymore and that knowledge crippled her. She missed kissing him, feeling his lips while they lay in her bed. She missed feeling his body on top of hers. His hands made her tremble with just the slightest touch. The thought of him brought her to tears.

Henry pulled away, anguish on his face. "I'm sorry. I'm so sorry. Please forgive me. It won't happen again."

"It's not you," she said quickly, wiping her tears away. "I'm sorry."

He looked down at her. "Please tell me what's bothering you. I don't even know what to do to help you."

"No."

"Do I have to beg? I will."

She clutched her body and tried to breathe through the pain. "I'm in love with Coen." His eyes widened but he said nothing. "We've been together for a month but when you told me how you felt about me, I couldn't tell you the truth—that I loved him. I didn't want to cause you any more pain because I love you so much. You're my family." She wiped her tears away and caught her breath. "When I refused to tell you about us, Coen got tired of being kept a secret. He felt like I didn't care about him enough to tell everyone I know that we were together—including you.

The party was my last chance but I still couldn't do that to you."

Henry looked away then ran his fingers through his hair. He said nothing, staring out across the ocean. Sydney knew she just broke his heart. Suddenly, he stood up and marched back to his car. She followed behind him until she caught up to him.

"Henry, I'm so sorry."

"Now that you told me the truth, can you get back together?"

She wasn't expecting that question. "He won't take me back," she said through her tears. "I lost him forever."

"You chose me over him?"

"You're my family."

He nodded then walked to his car.

"Where are you going?"

He said nothing as he slammed the door closed. He drove out of the driveway and disappeared. Now she lost two of the people she loved most in the world. She had no idea how Henry was taking the news. When he tried to kiss her, she broke down in tears. That was scarring enough. Now she broke his heart and Coen's. All she did was hurt the people she loved—over and over.

## 17

Sydney sat in the living room and stared at the wall for a long time. She'd lost everything she cared about. What was left? When the knock sounded on the door, she flinched. Since she was so curious about who could be visiting her, she decided to answer it. It obviously wasn't Henry or Coen.

When she opened the door, Henry walked inside and shut it behind him before she could even blink.

"Can I talk to you for a second?"

"Yeah," she said weakly.

He took her hand and guided her to the living room. When they sat down, he squeezed her hand and stared at it. "Sydney, I love you so much."

"I love you too."

"But I'm really hurt by what you did."

"I'm sorry. I shouldn't have let you kiss me. That was my fault."

"That isn't what I meant. You shouldn't have hid Coen from me like that."

"I was just trying to protect you."

"I know. I understand that." He looked at her. "But this has caused me so much more pain than what you tried to spare me from."

"What?"

"I can't believe you did this to yourself. You are in love with this guy so you should be with him, not me." Her eyes softened when she looked at him. "It's okay, Sydney. I'll be okay."

"It doesn't matter now anyway."

"I want you to be happy, not miserable. Seeing you practically dead this week was the worst pain I've ever endured. I would much rather see you with someone else, happy that you found the person you love. I'm not gonna lie. I wish it was me, but it's okay that it's not. You never should have put my happiness before your own."

She felt the tears fall. "You're so sweet to me."

"If the situation was reversed, you would feel the same way."

She nodded, knowing he was right.

"Are we okay?"

"I'm sorry about everything."

"Please don't lie to me like that ever again."

"I won't," she said quickly.

"I'm very happy for you," he said as he squeezed her hand.

"What do you mean?"

"I'm happy for you two."

"We aren't together anymore."

"Come with me." He pulled her to a stand and led her to the front door. He walked outside then stepped out of the way, moving to the side of the porch. She looked at Henry then spotted the other figure standing in the dirt. Coen had his hands in his pockets as he stared at her, a smile on his face.

"Coen?" she asked.

He walked up the steps and grabbed her face. "Baby?"

More tears started to fall. "I'm so sorry about everything."

"I forgive you."

"You shouldn't."

"You told him about me. That's enough for me." He rubbed his nose against hers. "And he told me what you said." She stared at him, her eyes wide. "That you're in love with me."

"I am."

"I'm in love with you too."

She breathed a sigh of relief. "I thought I lost you."

"You never could."

"But you left me."

"I was waiting for you, hoping you would just be honest with him. Now that I know you told him, I know you're serious about me. I know that you love me."

"I love you so much."

"I know you do."

She wrapped her arms around his neck and held him close. "Please don't ever leave me again. I wouldn't survive."

"I won't. I'm yours."

Henry averted his gaze then walked toward his car without saying goodbye. Sydney broke from Coen's embrace then followed him.

"Henry?"

"Yeah?" he said without turning out.

"I love you."

He took a deep breath. "I love you too."

"Thank you so much."

He played with his keys in his hands. "I want you to be happy."

Coen came beside her. "He's a good guy. I'm glad that he's your best friend."

"Bye," Henry said as he opened his car door.

Sydney walked around the vehicle then wrapped her arms around him. "I can't believe you did that."

"I can," he said as he held her close, trying to hide his tears.

She held him tightly, wanting to comfort him as much as possible.

"Now go be with him," he whispered. "I'll be fine."

She pulled away and kissed his tears away. "You always have a part of my heart, Henry."

He smiled. "Give it all to him, Sydney. I don't need it." He climbed into the car then started the engine without looking at her. He pulled out of the driveway and disappeared. Sydney stood there and watched him go.

Coen approached her and stood in front of her. "He'll be okay."

She looked at him. "What did he say to you?"

"He begged me to take you back."

Her eyes watered. "He did?"

"He told me he kissed you and you started crying, saying how much you loved me. As much as he loves you, he knows you'll never feel the same way. Now he can move on. It's the best thing that's ever happened to him. The last thing he wants is for you to worry about him. Please be happy."

She nodded. "He's so amazing."

"I like him too."

"You don't hate him for kissing me?"

He was quiet for a moment. "It's in the past."

"I can still be friends with him?"

"Best friends," he said. "After what he did, I have nothing but respect and trust for him. He behaved exactly as I predicted. And I trust you, baby."

"Thank you."

"You don't need to thank me."

She wrapped her arms around his neck and pressed her forehead against his. "I missed you so much. You have no idea."

"I do. Are you busy this weekend?"

"No."

"Good. Because I'm staying here all weekend. I brought my clothes."

"Really?"

"I haven't been able to sleep and I know you haven't either. We can catch up."

"I don't want to sleep," she whispered.

"Good. I didn't either." He pulled away and grabbed her hand. "There's something I want to show you."

"What?"

"You'll have to wait and see." He pulled her toward the beach. When they reached the sand, it was dark with the exception of a small flicker of light.

A blanket sat on the beach with candles surrounding it, forming the shape of a heart. The slight breeze made the candles shine bright then darken again. There was no one in sight of them. They had the entire place to themselves.

"Do you like it?"

"It's wonderful," she said as ran to it and sat down, looking at the candles then the ocean. "So beautiful."

He stepped over the line of candles then sat next to her, wrapping his arm around her shoulder. "I missed you."

"I missed you too," she said as she hugged him. Having him in her arms made her forget about all the pain and agony she experienced that week. She sighed peacefully.

"I hated ignoring you. It was the hardest thing I've ever had to do."

"I understand why you did it. I was wrong, Coen. I messed this up."

He kissed her forehead. "You are loyal to those you love. I understand that. You didn't mean to hurt me. You are just a very selfless person. I admire that about you."

"You do?"

"It's annoying sometimes but I still think you're amazing."

"I'm sorry about all the pain I caused you. I was being stupid."

"Let's forget about it. We're together now— finally."

"I love you."

He rubbed his nose against hers. "I love you too."

"Can you stay all week?"

He smiled. "I have to go home sometime."

"No, you don't."

"Be patient, baby. We'll get there."

209

"Okay." She lay down and pulled him with her. "I want to make out."

He chuckled. "I thought about kissing you all week."

She pulled him on top of her and pressed her lips against his. The tears started to fall as she felt his body lie on top of her, sheltering her. His lips fit perfectly against hers, molding to her mouth. His kiss was different, unconditional.

He pulled away then kissed her tears before he rubbed his nose against hers. "Why are you crying?" he whispered.

"Because I'm so happy."

"Well, I'm going to make you cry a lot then."

"I look forward to it."

He sealed his mouth over hers and kissed her again, running his fingers through her hair. It was silky and soft, smelling like coconut and vanilla. When he pressed his palm against her face, it was no longer wet with tears. She finally stopped crying. He leaned farther over her and pressed his hips against her, pushing his erection into her thigh.

Sydney moaned when she felt him. Their kisses turned passionate and heated within seconds, just like they always did. Even though the ocean was crashing against the shore, yelling with the sound of nature, neither one of them noticed. The water, sand, and trees disappeared to the back of their minds. All they thought about was each other, being with each other.

She ran her fingers under his shirt, feeling his warm body, sliding over every muscle. She felt safe with him in her life, like nothing would ever hurt her. That safety and that reassurance was something she had been missing for so long. She finally felt whole with him, complete. She pulled his shirt from his body then tossed it aside.

"I want to lose control," she whispered.

"I do too."

She unbuttoned his pants and slid them off, taking his boxers with them. Once he was naked, she kissed him again, darting her tongue into his mouth with heated breaths. Her hands grabbed his ass then felt the muscles of his back, wanting to touch him everywhere.

Coen let her explore while he kissed her, knowing his body made her more aroused than anything else ever did. When she reached down to his cock and rubbed him gently, he breathed into her mouth, his moans mixing with hers. Unable to hold on a moment longer, he pulled off her shirt and bra.

She gazed up at him with love in her eyes then reached down to unbutton her own pants.

"Slow," he said as he steadied her hands. "Slow. This is the first time I'm going to make love to you. I want it to be perfect."

"It already is."

He leaned down and sucked on each of her nipples, making her moan louder than a moment before. Her fingers glided through his hair and gripped him tightly. When he pulled away, he pinched each nipple while he looked her in the eye. She bit her lip as she watched him.

Finally, he pulled down her shorts, which she was eager to kick away. He removed her underwear then tossed it on the sand. He held himself over her while he looked down at her. She wrapped her legs around his waist then ran her hands up his chest.

"Coen," she whispered. "I've never been more turned on in my life."

He grabbed a sheet and pulled it over his ass, shielding both of their lower bodies, then leaned over her. When he pressed his lips against her, his kiss was slow and gentle. She shivered as she relished every touch of his mouth. It somehow made her even more aroused than before.

Coen grabbed her hips and tilted them slightly, giving him a better position over her. Her hands gripped his forearms as she waited for him to enter her. By the pressure of her fingers against his skin, he knew she was anxious to feel him. There wasn't a doubt in her mind that she wanted this. There wasn't a doubt in his.

He broke their kiss and stared into her eyes. Her lips were slightly open as she met his gaze. Her eyes were greener than they normally were, brighter and lusher with unseen landscapes. He didn't just see beauty and depth in her look, but everything he ever loved. He saw his whole world inside her. In that moment he knew wouldn't ever be apart from her. If there was someone he was destined to be with, it was her.

She rubbed her nose against his, trying to stop herself from begging him. The anticipation was killing her. She had wanted for this for so long. Initially, she just wanted to fuck him just like all the other girls. She wanted him to pound into her all night because she was horny and lonely, missing a man's touch, but now she wanted him for other reasons. She wanted to give herself to him so they could be united in that moment, sharing their souls with each other. Never in her life had she loved someone with her whole heart until now. She loved him and respected him, wanted him for as long as he would have her.

He pressed his tip against her entrance and she immediately gasped. Now she understood just how big he was. She knew it just by looking at him, but his head was barely moving inside of her. It was going to take some work to get the entire thing inside. She was just small from her temporary abstinence, but she knew she would enjoy their lovemaking as soon as she got used to it.

He looked into her eyes as he gently moved inside of her. Her breathing increased as his head slipped based her entrance. She gripped his forearms tighter because it felt so good. She hadn't been stretched like that in so long. She wanted more.

She placed her hand on his lower back and pulled him gently, asking him to go farther.

With a shaky breath, he moved further within her. His shaft was barely inside of her because she was so tight. It was like having sex with a virgin. She was so wet and warm that he wanted to come right then and there. He pressed his forehead against hers, biting his lip because it felt so good. They had barely started but he knew this would be the best sex he ever had. He had never been so in love with someone like he was with her. It was quick, happened within a month, but there wasn't a doubt in his mind that he loved this girl. He moved further inside.

A quiet gasp escaped her lips. He kissed her then kept moving. When he was halfway within her, he felt her stretch wide enough to allow him to move completely inside her. With one fluid motion, he inserted the rest of him.

"Coen," she said as she scratched his back.

He didn't move once he was inside her. The tightness was so pleasurable that he had to stop for a moment. Also, he wanted to give her time to adjust to him. "You okay?"

"Shut up," she said as she breathed into his mouth.

He started to rock into her gently, moving his entire length in then out of her. She breathed heavily as moved inside her, grabbing him and scratching him everywhere. When she opened her legs wider and started to rock him from below, he knew she was really enjoying it. He increased his pace then saw the color flood her cheeks. She was on the verge of coming and he could feel her tighten around him, preparing for the cataclysm of the orgasm.

Her lips opened and she moaned, screamed for him. "Coen."

He moved into her harder so she could enjoy it as much as possible. He remained in control so he wouldn't come too soon and ruin this perfect moment.

She was completely out of control. The pleasure was so much that she grabbed him everywhere, just to hold onto something as she exploded. It was the best sex she ever, the hardest orgasm, and the hottest sex she ever had. Gasping and moaning the entire time, she rode her wave until every last ounce of it was completely gone. "Oh my fucking god."

Coen was determined to give her another. He was going to be the best she ever had. He would make every other guy she screwed look like they didn't know what they were doing. It was going to be the most sensual and satisfying experience she ever had. After all the pleasure she gave him just from letting him inside her, he was going to make her legs shake.

"That was so good," she said as she grabbed the back of his neck.

He reached his hand down and started to rub her clit. The second orgasm was harder to reach but he was willing to rise to the challenge. He held himself up with one hand as he rocked to her, moving even harder than before. His thumb circled her clitoris hard and fast. He not only wanted to make her come hard, but fast. He couldn't last much longer. She was too beautiful, too gorgeous not to lose control. When her legs started to shake and she was moaning in his ear, saying incoherent things, he knew she was on the brink. His thrusts became hard as he moved into her. He liked this even more because she started to scream, yelling his name to everyone in their vicinity. The whales, the dolphins, the birds—everything heard her. Coen didn't mind and neither did she.

When the second explosion hit, it was somehow better than the first one. It circulated in her blood and touch every nerve ending, amplifying the pleasure tenfold. Her pussy was tender and pulsating with pleasure like the waves of an aftershock. It felt so good she thought she might have a third because the second one was so good.

Coen stared at her mouth, which formed in a circle as she howled for him, completely possessed by him. There was no one else in her thoughts but him, and he knew her heart was completely devoted to him. When she finished her moment, she gripped his shoulders and started to rock into him as he moved into her, increasing the pace. It felt so good he moaned loudly.

"Stop moving," she whispered.

He stopped moving his hips.

She rocked him from below, sheathing him repeatedly. Coen remained suspended over her, letting her wet and tight pussy fuck him from underneath. He gripped her neck as he watched her face as she moved into him. Sweat dripped from between her breasts as she moaned for him, loving the control. He tightened his hold on her as the orgasm started to form in the base of his balls. It was slow but steady, and increased before the final moment of release.

When he bit his lip, she knew he was about to come. His hand on her neck told her exactly where he was in the process. When he started to move into her hard and fast, she knew it was here. His breathing became deep grunts as he thrust into her. He closed his eyes as he felt himself explode.

He pulled out and started to come on her stomach. Sydney grabbed his shaft and started to jerk him off as hard as she could, making it last as long as possible. He pressed his forehead against hers as he squirted everywhere, coming more than he ever had in his life, even when he was teenager.

They were both out of breath when they were done, satisfied and exhausting from their lovemaking.

"You are so good at that," she said as she kissed his forehead.

"You make me good."

She kissed his lips. "That was so amazing."

He smiled, still breathing hard. "I'm glad you enjoyed it."

"Are you kidding me? I'm lucky if I come one, but twice? That was definitely the best sex I ever had."

"Don't get ahead of yourself. We still have a lot of sex to have."

"I look forward to it." She kissed his neck then his chest, tasting the sweat on his skin.

He moved away and lied down beside her. He grabbed the sheet and wiped her off. "Sorry about that."

"I don't mind at all."

"Please go on the pill. I hate condoms."

"I'm surprised you lasted so long."

"I jacked off before I came so I would last longer."

"How sweet."

He smiled. "I wanted this night to be a moment you would remember forever."

"It is."

"You wanna sleep out here?"

"As long as we do that again."

"We will."

"I'm on top this time."

His eyes widened. "I like the sound of that."

She cuddled next to him and looked at the stars while they listened to the waves of the sea. She had fallen apart so quickly without him by her side, and now everything was right again. Coen was everything to her; her family, her friend, her entire world. Now that he knew just how important he was to her, she had to tell him the truth— the whole truth.

Her past would come back and bite her in the ass and it was just better to be honest about it. Her stepfather was coming to the island for Thanksgiving, and Sydney wouldn't be able to hide his presence from Coen. When he knew the depth of her dark past, she hoped he wouldn't take off running. But tonight wasn't the night. Right now, they were the only two people looking up at those stars. Nothing else mattered.

The story continues....

# Breaking Through the Waves

(Book Two of the Hawaiian Series)

Available Now

# About the Author

E. L. Todd was raised in California where she attended California State University, Stanislaus and received her bachelor's degree in biological sciences, then continued onto her master's degree in education. While she considers science to be interesting, her true passion is writing. She is also the author of the *Soul Saga Trilogy, The Alpha Series, and her bestselling novel, Only For You, the first installment of the Forever and Always Series.* She is also an assistant editor at Final-Edits.com.

# By E. L. Todd

## Soul Catcher
(Book One of the Soul Saga)

## Soul Binder
(Book Two of the Soul Saga)

## Soul Relenter
(Book Three of the Soul Saga)

## Only For You
(Book One of the Forever and Always Series)

## Forever and Always
(Book Two of the Forever and Always Series)

## Edge of Love
(Book Three of the Forever and Always Series)

## Force of Love
(Book Four in the Forever and Always Series)

## Fight for Love
(Book Five in the Forever and Always Series)

## Lover's Roulette
(Book Six in the Forever and Always Series)

## Happily Ever After
(Book Seven of the Forever and Always Series)

# Sadie
(Book One of the Alpha Series

# Elisa
(Book Two of the Alpha Series)

# Connected by the Sea
(Book One of the Hawaiian Crush Series)

# Breaking Through the Waves
(Book Two of the Hawaiian Crush Series)

# Connected by the Tide
(Book Three of the Hawaiian Crush Series)

# Taking the Plunge
(Book Four of the Hawaiian Crush Series)

Made in the USA
Charleston, SC
16 April 2014